Flo—
It's been [illegible] you via em[illegible] enjoy the new book. It was a long time in coming.
Beth

IN MY DREAMS

Beth Mitchum

Here's hoping that all your GOOD dreams come true.
Beth Mitchum

UltraVioletLove Publishing

Poulsbo

Edited by Beth Mitchum
Cover and interior design by Beth Mitchum
Cover photo "Moonrise over Downtown Seattle" used with permission from Dreamstime.com. © **Philgophoto**
Cover photo of blue Honda Accord is a stock photo that was altered by Beth Mitchum.

Published by:
UltraVioletLove
PO Box 1681
Poulsbo, WA 98370
UltraVioletLovePublishing.com

UltraVioletLove Publishing chose CreateSpace.com as a conduit for publishing because of its print on demand technology. Only small quantities of this title will be printed as needed in order to cut back on the tremendous amount of waste generated by the book publishing industry. As an author-centered publishing house, all profits generated from the sale of our books go directly to the authors. UltraVioletLove Publishing is paid only for services rendered for editing and preparation of a book and its cover. For more information, check our website at UltraVioletLovePublishing.com.

Printed and bound in the United States of America

ISBN: 1438253761
EAN-13: 9781438253763

Dedicated to Karla.

You got me thinking
about the possibility
of dream worlds
colliding with reality.

I bet you didn't know that.

IN MY DREAMS

Beth Mitchum

Chapter 1
Stolen Moments

I sensed the thrill of a stolen moment as my fingers brushed back a lock of auburn hair that had fallen in front of her left eye. I cupped her face in my hand, gently tilting it up towards mine so that our eyes met. I saw in them a passion that seemed to echo the intensity I was experiencing and was thus emboldened to make the first move. When my lips landed softly on hers, I felt a surge of excitement and danger.

After a fleeting moment of bliss, she pulled away from me, wrenching her body from my embrace. Turning quickly, she knocked over the kitchen chair, on which she had been seated before she stood up to give me a hug.

"Why did you do that?"

Like a child caught misbehaving, yet in denial of the fact, I responded innocently. "What?"

"You kissed me! Why did you do that?"

"Oh, that."

"Yes, that! What else would I be referring to?"

I hung my head, shame filling the breast that had so recently felt bold and brave. "I'm sorry. I don't know what came over me. I thought... I felt... You looked..."

"I looked like what?"

I paused, took a deep breath, and then forged ahead. "I thought that you wanted me to kiss you."

"That I...? Whatever gave you that idea?"

"The look you gave me when I brushed the hair out of your eyes. It was soft and tender. It just felt right for me to kiss you. I'm sorry I startled you. Obviously I misinterpreted your body language. I won't do it again. In fact, I should just leave now." I turned and walked towards the door.

"Stop! I'm sorry. You're right. I did want you to kiss me. I-I don't know why. I don't know what's happening."

I turned back towards her and saw the look of pain and confusion in her eyes. I tilted my head to the side like an eager puppy. "You did want me to kiss you?"

"Yes," she whispered. She took two steps towards me and reached out her arms. "And I think I'd really like for you to do it again."

I walked into her waiting arms and gave her a warm, lush, passionate kiss. After a moment or two, I felt as though I were buzzing with all the electricity in our kiss. Then I realized that it wasn't me who was buzzing, but something in the background. It sounded like an alarm. Then it hit me.

I sat up in bed and slammed my hand down on the snooze bar. "Damn! It was just a dream!" I punched my pillow with great ferocity, exclaiming with each blow, "Shit! Shit! Shit!" I violently disentangled my limbs from the covers and pulled my nightshirt over my head. I stalked angrily to the bathroom and turned on the shower. I took a moment to pee in the toilet while the water warmed up then stepped under the spray of a disinterested showerhead.

After I was sufficiently scrubbed and shampooed, I stalked back to the bedroom and sat on the edge of the bed next to my ever-faithful sleeping companion, trying to calm myself. "I can't believe I had another dream about her," I whispered to my Cocker Spaniel, as I stroked her curly black fur. "I hardly know her. What is it about this woman that makes me keep dreaming about her? She's married, for goodness sake. She's probably never even dreamed about having a relationship with a woman. I've got to get a love life. A real love life. This is driving me out of my mind!"

I bent over and kissed Jolly on the head and thanked her for listening to the ravings of a sex-starved lesbian. Then I set my mind to the task of finding something to wear to work. I found myself judging my wardrobe on the basis of whether I thought Marie would think I looked sexy in it. Then I realized that she probably never even noticed what I wore to work. Although she had mentioned a couple times that she liked my polo shirt with the denim collar.

"Hmm. What do you think, Jolly, should I wear the denim work shirt? If she likes me in denim, this would certainly give her the full effect." Jolly wagged her tail at me, and I took that as confirmation. I slipped into my khaki chinos and tucked the denim shirt in, while I dug in the closet for my brown belt and boots. When I had completed my ensemble, I took a quick glance in the mirror to make sure nothing was out of place then headed to the kitchen for a bite of breakfast.

I made myself a cup of hot cocoa and poured a bowl of Raisin Bran from the box. Jolly followed me into the kitchen and looked sadly at her empty food bowl. I filled her food dish first then went to the fridge for some milk for my cereal. After I had finished eating, I rinsed my bowl and set it in the dishwasher. Looking satisfied and completely content with her lot in life, Jolly walked over to the doggy door and pawed at it. I unlocked it and patted her head as she went out for her morning romp in the backyard.

I switched on the television to find out what to expect from the weather on this Monday morning. I was hardly surprised when the forecast called for scattered showers throughout the Puget Sound region. What was spring in

Seattle, after all, without the April showers? I bid the weatherman a lovely day and grabbed my Gore-Tex jacket from the coat rack. I snatched my keys from the coffee table and exited the house, dead-bolting the door behind me.

While I defrosted the windshield and warmed up the engine of my green Honda Civic hatchback, I searched the radio waves for something other than morning talk shows. I finally found the light jazz station and melted into the upholstery as I recognized the rich tones of Randy Crawford. "Randy, you have such a sexy voice. Why don't you stop by my house tonight for a little wine and romance?"

When she didn't respond, I backed the car out of the driveway and headed for the office. I am fortunate in the fact that my work commute is short, if not exactly sweet. I do not have to get anywhere near the freeways in order to get to my place of employment. After less than ten minutes of back street driving, I pulled into the driveway of Renton Honda, my home-sweet-home away from home. I waved at Dave, a salesman I went to high school with, and then zoomed around back to find a parking spot.

I pulled up next to Marie's dark blue Accord sedan. My heart jumped into my throat when I realized she was still sitting in her car. She was wiping her eyes with a tissue. I walked over to make sure she was all right. She turned towards me and smiled a heart-stopping smile then opened her car door.

I leaned towards her over the car door and tried to catch her eye. "You okay, Marie?"

"Sure, Jill, why do ask?" She responded in her sexy, silky Latino voice. She slipped out of her car, shutting and locking the door behind her. She hung her leather purse strap over her shoulder.

I reached out to help her with the stack of files she was trying to juggle along with her keys and coffee mug. "I just thought that maybe you'd been crying or something." I took her commuter mug from her so she wouldn't spill her drink on the lovely burgundy dress that was peeking out from between the lapels of her trench coat.

She turned back towards me and blinked a couple times. "No, I got something in my eye this morning. It's been driving me crazy. I hope whatever it was didn't scratch the cornea."

My stomach did a backwards somersault, landing slightly off balance, as I remembered that this morning's dream had started when I helped Marie remove something from her eye. That was how we had found ourselves in an intimate situation. I sat her down in a chair in her kitchen and removed a dark speck with a Q-tip. Then she stood up and gave me a prolonged hug. Without stepping back, she had looked up at me, and in that moment the lock of hair had fallen into her eyes. I sighed and bowed my head as I relived the intensity of that dream kiss.

"Jill, are you all right?"

I looked up, startled by Marie's question. "I, yeah, sure, I'm okay. I was just remembering something."

"Well, it sure looked like an entrancing memory. I thought that you were having an out of body experience there for a minute." She hooked her arm through mine and started walking me towards the building where we both worked.

I laughed nervously. "Yeah, I guess you could say that. I was just recalling a dream I had this morning."

She stopped walking abruptly and tugged at my arm, turning me towards her. I stopped in my tracks as she looked at me suspiciously. "Anything you would care to share?"

I stuffed one fist in my pocket and barely stopped myself in time before I accidentally took a sip of Marie's coffee. I cleared my throat and shifted my weight a bit to one side. "Um, well, actually, you were in it."

The look Marie gave me in response was more of an accusing stare. "Oh?"

"Yeah. It's kind of weird because I was over at your house for some reason, though I have no idea what your house looks like. You know how dreams are. Anyway, you had gotten something in your eye, and I helped you get it out." Marie looked at me with an expression that could only be described as astonishment. "Marie?"

"I don't believe this," she said, almost to herself, taking a step backward.

"What?"

"I had a similar dream, only we were in your house, or what I presumed to be your house, since it didn't resemble my house in the least."

"Now wait a minute. Are you telling me that we had the same dream?"

"Sounds like it." Marie's face reddened a bit.

I ran my hand through my hair and expelled a really long breath. "So did anything else happen in your dream?"

Marie looked down at the ground then started walking quickly towards the office. "Um, yeah, there was a little bit more, but that's kind of fuzzy."

I stood there for a second or two, stunned by this revelation. Then I trotted after her, being careful not to spill her coffee. "So when did you get something in your eye?"

"I don't know. Five o'clock maybe. I had gotten up to say goodbye to Enrico, and when I got back into bed for a little more sleep, I felt something gritty in my eye. I guess it must've gotten incorporated into my dream."

"That makes plenty of sense to me. What doesn't make sense is that I should have the same dream."

"Yes, that is truly odd."

When we got to the door, I reached around Marie and pulled it open and held it for her. She turned and smiled almost coquettishly at me. I nearly let go of the door. Recovering in time, I managed to re-establish my grip before I completely lost it. Marie paused for a moment then started walking down the hallway towards her office. I opened that door for her too, handed her the coffee mug, and then continued on my way to the parts department, my mind filled with questions, my heart filled with conflicting emotions.

I tried all morning to put aside the memory of the dream. Yet it seemed to linger in the air like the scent of a smoldering campfire. When lunchtime arrived, I decided to walk to the deli for a sandwich. I nearly bumped into Marie as I started past the door to her office.

"Oh, Jill! Hi there. I'm sorry I almost knocked you down. I wasn't looking where I was going."

"That's okay. Are you off to lunch?"

"Yeah, I thought I'd grab a bite at the deli."

"What a coincidence. I was heading that way myself. Mind if I join you?"

Marie hesitated momentarily then responded almost too casually, "Um, sure. Why not?"

Marie pushed through the door ahead of me. I looked over her head out into the daylight. I was pleasantly surprised to find that wherever the scattered showers were today, they were definitely not over Renton at the moment. The sun was beaming down warmly on us. As we walked, I noticed that Marie looked a bit uncomfortable. Finally I said, "Look, is there something wrong? Would you rather not have lunch together?"

Marie paused and looked intently at me. "No, I'm all right, I guess."

"Is it the business about the dream?"

"I don't know. Maybe. Yes, I guess it is."

"That wasn't really a multiple choice question, you know." I smiled, thinking that it would be amazing if she really had experienced the same dream as mine.

Marie smiled at me and laughed. As we started walking again, she said, "No, I suppose not. I just can't seem to get it out of my mind. The dream, I mean."

"I know. I've been thinking about it all morning. It's pretty weird really. I've never had anything like that happen to me before."

"Well, that's the thing I don't understand, Jill. I have a history of having weird dreams. Dreams that predict things that end up happening later."

"What kind of things?"

"All kinds of things. Babies being born to women who aren't pregnant yet. People dying of illnesses that haven't yet been diagnosed. Car accidents before they happen."

"Whoa! That's pretty strange. I don't mean to be pushy, but what else was in your dream? I mean since it has to do with me and all?"

Marie blushed visibly. "You first."

"I, well, after I got the speck out of your eye, we, um, you know, sort of kissed. Then you got mad at me. Then we kissed again. Now it's your turn."

Marie started walking a little bit faster, as though she wished to run away from me. "Yeah, well, that pretty much sums up my dream too."

"Really?" I tried to get her to look me in the eye, but she avoided my glance.

"Yes, really." A lock of her hair became dislodged from its place behind her ear and dropped like a theater curtain between us. We walked along in silence until we reached the deli. I opened the door for Marie then followed her inside.

After we received our orders, we sat down at one of the tables. When I took a bite of my corned beef on rye, I noticed that Marie was staring at me. "What?" I said when my mouth wasn't so full.

"I'm sorry, Jill, but I am very confused about all this. I don't understand what is happening. I don't know where that dream came from, and I don't know what to do about it."

I looked at Marie's worried expression and smiled a reassuring smile. "Look, we both had the same dream. Sure, that's a strange coincidence. Obviously you're somewhat sensitive to psychic energy, but it doesn't necessarily mean that it's prophetic. Weird perhaps but not necessarily something that has to come true. Okay? So stop worrying about it and eat your lunch. You're thin enough without skipping meals. It's not good for you, you know."

"What's not good for me?" she asked, looking distracted.

"Worrying for one thing and not eating for another." I dabbed my mouth with my napkin. "Come on, I'm not going to attack you, Marie. I don't even know you that well. Chalk the dream up to indigestion, a weird hormonal blip, or whatever. But please stop worrying about it. I'm lesbian, yes, but you, you're straight and married. End of discussion."

"But that's just it, Jill. I'm not exactly straight." She practically whispered the last two words.

"What?" I barely managed to say without choking on my sandwich.

"Well, I guess I am now, but in college I wasn't."

"Are you telling me that you used to be lesbian?"

"I wasn't exclusively lesbian."

"Bisexual then?"

"Shh!" She looked around at the other customers in the restaurant, none of whom appeared to be aware of our existence. "That would be more accurate, though I actually thought I would end up settling down with a woman one day until I met Enrico. He came along during a period in my life when I was really depressed. He made me laugh. We became good friends. Then he asked me to marry him, so I did. That was the end of any other relationships with men or women."

"So, just how involved did you get in college?"

She shot me a look of exasperation. "Let's just say that I have a T-shirt from a gay pride parade that says, 'I can't even march straight.'"

I leaned towards her with a big smirk on my face. "You're kidding me!"

"No, I most certainly am not. But don't you see? I have these prophetic dreams sometimes, and I don't want this one to come true!"

"Gee, thanks!" I sat back in my seat, feeling my ego instantly deflate.

"It's not you, Jill. It's Enrico. He's a decent man in his own way, and I do care for him. We've had our rough spots, but we work it out. I don't want us to split up."

"So who says you have to split up? Who says the dream has to come true? Maybe it was just you picking up on my energy, incorporating it into your dreams."

Marie stopped in mid-thought and smiled coyly at me. "Is that a less than subtle way of telling me that you're attracted to me?"

I choked on my sandwich, reached for a second napkin to wipe my mouth, and knocked my Dr. Pepper onto the floor, all in a space of a few seconds. As I squatted down to wipe up my mess, a young man walked over, mop in hand, and cleaned up the puddle before I could wrestle another napkin out of the overfilled dispenser on our table.

"Thank you," I mumbled in his direction.

He smiled and nodded. I had to wonder if he'd been listening to our conversation. As I sat back down in my chair, I looked at Marie. She was smiling boldly at me. "I'll take that as a yes."

I took another bite of my sandwich and hid my face in my free hand while I painstakingly chewed and swallowed. When I looked up again, Marie was still sitting there beaming at me. It seemed to me that she was enjoying herself a great deal at my expense. Finally I managed to whisper, "Well, maybe just a little bit."

Marie proceeded to wolf down her sandwich and potato chips, smiling all the while.

After we had finished eating, we cleaned up our debris and headed back over to the office. As we strolled along, it suddenly hit me that for a woman who had been very displeased about her potentially prophetic dream, Marie had rather swiftly transformed into a contented soul.

"Um, I take it by the pleased look on your face that you're glad that I'm attracted to you?"

She smiled at me. "Why certainly. Everyone likes to be attractive to other people."

"And you don't mind being attractive to a lesbian?"

"Of course not. Why should I?"

"I don't know. You just seem to have gone from being disheartened to being delighted in a very small space of time. What exactly did I miss?"

"You didn't miss anything. I'm just feeling good about myself right now, and I'm not going to worry about the dream. It doesn't do any good anyway. If it's going to happen, then it's going to happen. I can't exactly stop it."

I stopped in my tracks and stared after her, my mouth hanging open slightly. "What's that supposed to mean? Don't you think people have free will? Don't you think we have a choice about the outcome of our lives?"

Marie stopped and turned back towards me. "I suppose so, but it just seems that every time I have one of those dreams, it comes true."

"What do you mean by 'one of those dreams?' Do all your dreams come true? How do you know which ones are supposed to be prophetic and which ones are just dreams?"

"It's just a feeling I get. I don't know how to explain it. I was trying to talk myself into believing it wasn't prophetic, until you told me that you'd had the same dream."

"I don't get it. You think this dream will come true just because I had a similar one?"

Marie put her hands on her hips and glared at me as though I were completely out of it. "The same dream, Jill. Shall we compare them a little more closely? Tell me everything you remember in as vivid detail as you can manage."

I cleared my throat nervously. "Okay, well, as I recall it, I was getting something out of your eye. You were sitting in a chair in a kitchen that wasn't mine, but I thought was yours. Then you stood up and gave me a hug for getting it out for you. Instead of releasing me, you leaned your head back and looked up into my eyes. I thought your eyes were communicating passion to me, so I brushed a lock of your hair back then leaned over and kissed you on the lips.

"After we kissed for a moment, you pulled away from me abruptly, knocking over the chair in the process. Then you asked me what I was doing. I mumbled something about thinking that you had wanted me to kiss you. You acted very offended, so I backed off, apologized, and started to leave."

Marie interrupted my tale by saying, "Then I came to my senses and realized that I had been silently willing you to kiss me. When I told you that, I also told you that I wanted you to kiss me again."

Suddenly uncomfortable, I started walking briskly towards the office.

Marie came up quickly beside me as we arrived at the back door to the office. "You tell it in such a dispassionate fashion, but for me it was a very hot dream. To be honest, Jill, it had a strong impact on me. I awoke feeling intoxicated, and now, now I am overwhelmed by my desire to have that kiss."

Not wanting to look into her eyes, I glanced at my watch then slid down to sit on the sidewalk to catch my breath and sort out my thoughts. Marie leaned over me, mussed my hair, and then went inside.

"How can you say that to me and then just walk away?" She couldn't hear me, of course, though I hoped she was psychic enough to sense my confusion.

I finally gathered up my wits enough to return to my office. I found a piece of scratch paper and wrote these words: "How could you say something like that then leave me sitting there?" I signed it "J." I walked over to Marie's office and stuck my head in to see if she was around. She wasn't at her desk, so I folded the note in half, wrote her name on it, and tucked it into the corner of her desk calendar. I retreated back to my office before she could return to catch me in the act.

About ten minutes later, while I had my ear attached to the phone listening to someone complain about bad windshield wiper blades, Marie stuck her head in the door. When she saw that I was on the phone, she winked then put a slip of paper down on my desk. It was folded. I motioned for her to wait a minute, but she shook her head at me and vanished back into the hallway.

When I had finally managed to extricate myself from the phone, I snatched up the piece of paper and opened it. It read: "See you in my dreams." I dropped the paper as though it had burned me. I ran both hands through my hair then glanced in the mirror across the room to check on my appearance. As I suspected, that motion had made my short blonde hair stick up on my head in distinctly rooster-like fashion. I pulled a comb from my desk drawer, set my wild hairs back in place, and started pacing back and forth. The phone rang before I was able to wear a hole in the carpet.

After what felt like the longest afternoon of my life, five o'clock finally arrived. I picked up the note and slipped it into my jacket pocket then hurried out to see if I could beat Marie to her car. When I got to my car, I was disappointed to find hers already gone. I pulled the note out and read it again, trying to figure out what it meant. Did she really think we might have the same dream again? Or a different dream that we both shared? Was something like that even possible? Or was she just flirting with me?

As I made my way home, I finally decided that Marie was just teasing me about my crush on her. Perhaps she was just enjoying being wanted by me and was going to play it for all it was worth. Well, so be it. Two could play that game. I would just enjoy the fact that she was happy that I found her so attractive.

Chapter 2
Wet Dreams

I stood in front of Marie's house debating the sanity of approaching her at home. *What if Enrico answers the door? What would I say to him?* When I raised my hand to knock, the door suddenly swung open before me, as though by an invisible butler.

I walked cautiously into the foyer of the house. I sensed that the door was closing behind me. "Hello? Is anyone home? Marie?"

Her rich, sexy voice whispered behind me, "You finally made it. I've been waiting for you. What took you so long?"

"You knew I was coming?"

"I didn't know for sure, but I was hoping you would come. I did, after all, invite you."

"You did?"

"Yes, don't you remember?"

"Uh, no, not exactly."

"Didn't you read my note?"

"What note?"

"The one I gave to you at work today, silly." She walked around me and looked at me, grinning playfully.

"Oh, the one that said, 'See you in my dreams?'"

"Of course. Now here you are in my dream."

"This is a dream?"

"Yes. Don't you remember this house? It's the same as the one from last night."

I scanned the room and was startled to find that it was indeed the same room I had been in when Marie and I had exchanged that second, most explosive kiss, the one that had been interrupted by my alarm clock. "Oh my god! It is. You mean this isn't your house?"

"Of course not, and neither is it yours. It is our house, our dream house, you might say."

"Um, okay. So you said you'd been waiting for me. What did you have in mind?"

Marie gave me a look that was filled with both derision and passion, all at the same time. "You are so naïve, Jill. We are here to make our dreams come true, to consummate the passion between us."

My stunned look of stupidity must have amused her, for she burst out laughing and offered to fix me a drink. I paused for a moment, wondering if drinking in my dreams would give me a hangover the next day. Finally I shook my head. "No thanks. If we're here to be passionate, I want to have my wits about me. I don't want to dampen any part of this with an alcoholic stupor."

Marie smiled seductively. "Well, I'm afraid I've already had a couple drinks while I was waiting for you. I was beginning to think you weren't going to show up. Besides, I thought I might need a little help getting loosened up."

When I looked into her eyes, I began to feel my body temperature rising. I could almost feel flames licking at my feet. I hoped I wouldn't do something totally bizarre, like spontaneously burst into flames. With this being a dream, there was no telling what could happen.

"How long have you been waiting for me?" I asked, slipping out of my jacket, noting that Marie looked pretty darned loose already.

Marie snatched the jacket from my hand and hung it on the back of one of the kitchen chairs. When she turned back towards me, I noticed that several of the buttons on her black silky shirt were unbuttoned. For a fleeting moment I wondered what I'd gotten myself into. Fear mixed with anticipation ripped through my body, as an adrenal wave of lust washed over me. I guess I must've been staring at Marie's fairly open blouse because she giggled and unbuttoned another button.

I felt myself blushing, as I caught a glimpse of her light brown skin in the ever-widening gap between the lapels of her top. Another wave of lust crashed over me. I felt Marie smiling at me so I looked up at her eyes. She had a look of complete and utter daring on her face. This was a woman who was obviously determined to enjoy herself. She turned her back towards me and unbuttoned enough buttons to allow her to slide her blouse halfway down her arms. Her shoulders lay bare beneath the thick locks of dark, wavy hair.

I heard someone gasp then blushed again when I realized it was me. She unbuttoned another button or two and let her blouse slide off her body onto the floor. I stood there rooted to the carpet beneath my feet. Desire battled with despair. I had wanted Marie in a calm, detached sort of way for so long, I was afraid of releasing my detachment. Yet I knew that I really wanted to see the breasts that were awaiting me a mere yard away, if only I could convince my feet to move.

Finally I managed to take a step towards her. She scooped up all her hair and piled it on top of her head, letting it slip slowly through her fingers. I gazed upon the exquisite curve of her neck and shoulders as the locks of hair cascaded down, obscuring the view of sheer beauty.

I took another step towards her. I leaned over and softly kissed the top of Marie's head. Since she was a good six inches shorter than me, this was easy to do. I ran my hands down both sides of her head, enjoying the silky feeling of her full-bodied hair. She leaned back against me and afforded me an overhead view of her bared chest. Her nipples were large and very dark. Her breasts, while not exactly huge, looked substantial enough to fill the palms of both my hands.

The wave of lust that washed over me in that moment was powerful enough to burst forth from my mouth in a deep-throated groan. To say that I love women is to understate my feelings completely. More accurately, I worship women, their bodies, their passion, their psyches. I do not look upon them as sex objects; I immerse myself in their beauty and the utter perfection of their individuality.

Relationships may require work, but passion requires only permission to indulge. Permission to release the inner streams of desire. I savored the smell of Marie's hair for a moment. It smelled of herbs and of the earth. Then she turned towards me and I leaned down to drink thirstily from the wine of her mouth. As her lips parted and our tongues met and entwined, I felt Marie's body melt into my embrace. My hands stroked the nakedness of her back; my fingers entangled themselves playfully in the strands of her hair.

I felt, rather than heard, the moan that escaped from Marie's chest. It was virtually subsonic, but the vibrations of it pounded against my chest. I pushed her away just far enough so that I could kneel before her, capturing her honey-flavored breasts in my mouth. She shuddered. I encircled her nipples with my tongue and ran my hands lightly over her shoulders and ribcage.

"Oh my God!" Marie exclaimed, as she slid her hands to her skirt. She unbuttoned the single button and unzipped the zipper. When she let go of the zipper, her skirt fell noiselessly to the floor.

I nearly fainted when I saw that she wore nothing beneath her skirt. I closed my eyes and inhaled the musky scent of her excited body. Then I sunk down farther towards the floor and allowed my mouth to approach the temple of her body. I worshipped this woman as only a lesbian can worship another woman. Her shouts of exultation filled the sanctuary of our dream house as our bodies and souls blended into oneness.

When she could stand no further acts of libation, the goddess Marie lifted up my countenance towards her and smiled upon me. She blessed me with her kisses, and I basked in the glory of her utter loveliness.

Then it happened. Her look of lust engulfed my heart. As her eyes burned into mine, I realized that detachment was no longer an option. I was falling in love with this woman. Hard and heavy was the fall.

Marie's small hands raised me to a standing position. She led me over to the soft leather couch in the living room of our dream home. She urged me gently into a horizontal position then kneeled on the floor beside me. She paused. My heart skipped a beat. I was suddenly afraid that she was going to flinch at making love to me. When I looked at the desire that poured from her eyes, I was equally afraid that she wasn't going to refrain from reciprocating.

She began to pull my sweatshirt over my head, so I sat up and made it easier for her. She pushed me back again gently yet firmly. She was communicating to me that she was the one in control here. I responded to her subliminal messages with eager submissiveness. If this woman wanted to have her way with me, then so be it. She was, after all, a goddess. Who was I, a mere mortal, to thwart her plans?

Since I don't wear a bra, Maria was free to caress my breasts at will. Yet she didn't touch me. She just sat there looking at my semi-nakedness, hands folded in her lap. Then as if she were a painter who had spotted a problem with her

work of art, she frowned. "You are still overdressed, Jill."
Then she reached over and unzipped my jeans. But instead of
taking them off, she seemed to be utterly overwhelmed by her
desire. She reached her hand into my pants and began
weaving her fingers in my pubic hair, moving ever closer to
the doorway of my soul.

Impatient with the results of this initial foray, she pulled
her hand out again and began to tug at my pants legs. She
stood up and leaned over the arm of the couch. She took off
my sneakers and socks then gently pulled my jeans off,
allowing them to land in a heap on the floor. Still not
completely satisfied with her work, she peeled off my
underwear with the skilled hand of a practiced lesbian lover.

When she had completed the task of disrobing me, she
returned to her original kneeling position on the floor beside
me. At that moment, the goddess smiled. Then she kissed my
hipbone. I looked curiously at this diminutive woman at my
side. Her hands began to caress every inch of my body. It felt
almost as though her hands were sculpting my body, shaping
it to suit her fancy. I yielded to her masterful strokes. Then
she rolled me over and began shaping my backside.

When she began to sculpt the insides of my thighs, she
got on top of me and wedged her knee between my legs. I
moved them farther apart to allow her access to the fountain
that flowed from my body. I trembled as her fingers drew
closer and closer to the source of the waves that were crashing
upon the sand-colored thighs beneath her. As her small hand
entered my body, I felt as though I was being filled with the
spirit of life itself. Her kneading caress stroked the walls of
my temple, causing them to weep with joy and happiness.

I yielded to her expert ministrations, allowing my spirit
to soar on the wings of eagles. We soared up into the sky and
then beyond into the vast expanse of the galaxy. As her hands
fondled me, inside and out, I collided with a meteor and
exploded into a million pieces of stardust. Those bits and

pieces coalesced into a star, only to be shattered by an oncoming comet. Once the pieces pulled themselves together after the second explosion, they were then rammed by a starship, the USS Marie. This final encounter resulted in a fiery ball of liquid that flowed onto the couch beneath my shaken body.

I stumbled from the wreckage of my body and looked into her eyes. They were smiling at me — me, Jill, worshipper of the goddess Marie. I gazed into the light in her eyes, and I saw that it was good.

Contented, I closed my eyes and drifted back out into space. When I opened them again, I was in my own bed alone. My bed covers were strewn across the bed, as though someone had torn them from my sleeping body. Not even Jolly had managed to weather the storm that had torn through my dreams that night.

I noticed a damp spot on the bed beneath me when I got up to relieve the pressure on my bladder. I smiled as I remembered the contents of my dream. I reached down and felt the trickle that continued to flow from my body. I moaned in pleasure, still feeling drunk from the wine that had flowed from Marie's mouth. My heart was full to overflowing with love and passion for Marie.

I stumbled on trembling legs to the bathroom. It had been a while since I'd had sex that left me feeling this spent. I thought eagerly about seeing Marie the next day. On the return trip from the bathroom, I ran into Jolly. She wagged her tail at me sleepily and followed me back into the bedroom. She curled up on the floor, as though afraid to be rocked again by the explosions that had been caused by my earlier dreams.

I smiled at her, straightened out the covers a little bit, and then slipped into bed rolling away from the damp spot on the sheets. I closed my eyes and tried to recover the sense of reverie, if not the actual dream. I drifted back off to sleep. This time it was a dreamless sleep.

When I awoke again, it was dawn. My alarm clock had not yet gone off, so I lay there for a while thinking about what I would say when I saw Marie today. I had an uneasy feeling about how I could address the dream of the night before. Somewhere in between anticipation of today and the memories of last night was a fear that I was the only one who'd had the dream. Perhaps I dreamed it because of what she said, while she had slumbered the night through without an inkling of what was going on inside me. Only time would tell, and at the moment time was telling me to get up and get ready for work before I fell asleep again.

Chapter 3
Morning Aftermath

After a leisurely shower, I took advantage of the extra time I had from getting up early to fix myself a big breakfast. I caught myself whistling as I scrambled two eggs and poured them into the frying pan. I was feeling great. I'd just had the best sex of my life the night before. Never mind that it had all been a dream. It had been vivid enough to make me feel satisfied and in love with the whole world. Suddenly the entire universe felt like a hospitable place in which to dwell.

Even the sun had decided to come out this morning. I hadn't seen much of that bright shining star in the past six months, so I took it as a sign that the solar system had aligned itself to match my mood. When I got into my car and turned on KWJZ, the DJ told me that this was no mere sun break I was experiencing. This sun was going to shine on me all day. Then they played an older song by Alana Davis that was my one of favorites. I drove along singing and grooving with her sexy, soulful voice in my ears. All was right with the world.

When I pulled into the parking lot, I wasn't surprised to find that I had beaten Marie to work. I had gotten up nearly an hour earlier than usual. Even with the leisurely pace I had taken with my morning routine, I was still nearly ten minutes early. I locked my car and strode into the building, whistling the whole way. As I passed my friend, Dave, he gave me a puzzled look. "What happened to you?"

"What do you mean?"

"You look like a woman who has just won the lottery and are on your way to turn in your resignation."

"Do I? Hmm, well, I feel almost that good. No, I feel better than that." I flashed him a grin and shut the door to my office behind me. I peeked through the glass window and saw him shake his head and walk towards the sales offices. I mentally patted myself on the head and got to work immediately. I lost track of the time because I was so involved in my work. When I finally looked up at the clock I was startled to find that it was already eleven. I decided to take a quick break and head for the water cooler, knowing that I would have to pass Marie's desk en route.

As I entered the room, I noticed that Marie's desk was uncluttered and that her chair was pushed in. It looked as though she'd never even touched it today. Puzzled, I asked the woman at the desk next to Marie's if she'd been there today. She shook her head without looking up. "She called in sick this morning. Something about a family illness. Left me with lots to do, so I hope she's back tomorrow."

I nodded and backed out the door, completely forgetting my need for refreshment. I had water in my office anyway, but I sometimes went to the cooler to stretch my legs. That's how my acquaintance with Marie had begun. I had known her for nearly a year, though not very well. We exchanged pleasantries for a while until one day I ran into her on the way to lunch. We ended up going together and had enjoyed an interesting and lively conversation about nothing in particular. Since then we had gone to lunch about once every other week or so. Nothing planned, mostly just chance encounters that seemed to happen rather frequently.

After a couple months of this, I had begun trying to catch her attention on my way to the water cooler. The chance encounters turned into planned events. All the planning was on my part, of course. Then I started fantasizing about her. Then I started dreaming about her. Then we both had that dream. Now I was back to wondering if I had just made everything up in my head. Surely she wouldn't skip work if she had experienced last night's dream as well.

I wanted to call her, but I didn't think that would be particularly smart. What if Enrico answered? Then I shook my head in an attempt to clear the emotional clutter from my thought processes. *So what if Enrico answered the phone? If I had to identify myself, I could simply tell him that I heard she might be having some problems and wanted to offer my support. Friends and co-workers do that sometimes. There was nothing suspicious or weird about that.*

I looked up her number in the phone book. It was there, listed under Enrico Garcia. How very quaint and traditional. It annoyed me to think about women who jettisoned the last names of their family of origin. I wondered what else she had given up in order to marry this guy. I knew now, of course, that she had given up women, which, I think, is really what was bothering me about her taking on his last name. What did this man have to offer her that a woman couldn't? Children? Penetration? A lesbian could always strap one on, if that kind of penetration is what switches on her love light, and there is more than one way to build a family these days.

Annoyed at my own frustration, I threw the phone book on the desk. *Damn! This is ridiculous. Just call the woman. You haven't done anything to feel guilty about. People aren't morally responsible for what happens in their dreams. If you murdered someone in your dreams, you couldn't be arrested for it. No crime committed, no harm done.*

I dialed the number and waited as it rang two, three times. Finally a male voice answered, "Hello?"

"Yes, um, hello. Is Marie there?"

"Who is this?"

"My name is Jill. I'm Marie's co-worker. I heard—"

"Jill? Did you say your name was Jill?" The man on the other end of the line sounded extremely angry.

"Uh, yes, Jill. I—"

"Marie!" The man, who I presumed must be the charming Enrico, screamed too close to the mouthpiece. "The phone's for you. It's Jill! Did you hear that? A deep-voiced woman named Jill."

I cringed as I listened to the sarcasm and anger in the man's voice as he unleashed a torrent of Spanish words I couldn't follow but instinctively knew spelled trouble. I could hear Marie's voice in the background saying, "Jill is on the phone? Jill who?"

I nearly hung up the phone, but I felt almost mesmerized by the drama being played out at the other end of the line.

"She says she works with you. I thought you said you didn't know anyone named Jill."

My heart stopped. My breathing stopped. I couldn't figure out what had happened, but I knew that something was terribly wrong, and I felt as though I were to blame for it somehow. I held my breath.

"Oh, Jill from the office. I wonder what she wants."

"Well, I guess you'd better find out. You're keeping your little friend waiting."

I didn't like the way he said "little friend." It sounded condescending. It sounded threatening, menacing even. It definitely didn't sound right, whatever it was.

Then suddenly Marie was on the phone.

"Hello?" Her voice sounded small and frightened.

"Marie? It's Jill."

"Jill, what a surprise. Is something wrong at work?"

"No, I, I'm sorry to bother you at home. It's just that Candace said you were having family trouble or something, and I just wanted to check on you. Are you all right?"

"Of course I'm all right," she said none too convincingly. "Don't worry."

"Are you sure?"

"Yes, I'm sure. I'm fine, just fine. Tell Candace I'll be back tomorrow and everything will be as it was before."

"Uh, okay, whatever. Sorry to bother you."

"Thank you so much for being concerned about me. Thank Candace too. You girls are so kind to me. Thanks for calling. Bye now."

The phone went dead in my ear. I look at the mouthpiece and said aloud, "Liar."

Just as I did this, my boss passed by my open door and looked down his nose over the glasses that were perched there. "Is everything all right, Ms. Michaels?"

"Yes, sir. Everything is just fine."

"Was that a customer you were talking to?"

"No, actually I wasn't talking to anyone really. Just a dead phone line."

He scratched his head and peered intently at me. "I see," he said, though clearly he had no idea what to make of my actions. No more a clue than I did as to what had just transpired on the phone. Then he nodded and continued walking down the hall.

I returned the phone to its cradle and tried to think of a plausible reason why Enrico would be so angry because of that phone call. He had seemed okay until I told him my name. I glanced at the clock and noticed that it was getting close to lunchtime. I decided to get the hell out of there so I could figure out what was going on with Marie. I put on my jacket and sunglasses and headed out for a sunny lunch.

I pushed the door open to walk outside and found that the sky had begun to darken, and the clouds overhead threatened rain. *So much for the sun shining on me all day.* I guess it wasn't just the weather that had taken a turn for the worse. Something was definitely wrong with Marie, and if that phone call were any indication, I wouldn't be learning anything more about it until tomorrow.

Chapter 4

Annoying the Dog

That night I slept restlessly, constantly tossing and turning, sighing and groaning. After a couple hours of this, Jolly sighed, got down from the bed, and curled up on the floor. When I got up for a third trip to the bathroom, I noticed that she had gone out to sleep on the couch. It was the first time in the five years we had been together that she hadn't slept in the same room with me. I was feeling so disturbed I was even beginning to annoy my dog.

Around four in the morning, I got up to find something to read. Nothing sounded interesting enough to get my mind off Marie. Finally I drifted off into a state of exhaustion that left no room for dreams, only deep, snoring slumber. When the alarm went off, I awoke feeling as though an army of sweaty soldiers had camped in my mouth. I had to brush my teeth before I could even think about eating anything. I felt awful, completely drained, devoid of any emotion except disgust with myself and life in general.

Jolly attempted to engage my attention, but when I just smiled wanly at her, she tucked her tail and went to the bedroom. I turned on the radio, hoping to find some music that might perk me up enough to help me get ready for work. First I came across "Only Love Can Break Your Heart." I quickly changed the station. I paused when I heard Elton John's voice, but groaned when I realized it was his old duet with Kikki Dee, "Don't Go Breaking My Heart." There was no doubt in my mind that my heart was already breaking. What was the point of reinforcing it with the song lyrics of perfect strangers?

I turned off the stereo and opted instead to listen to the droning sounds of the morning news shows. That move backfired on me though, since I fell asleep at the breakfast table, mesmerized by the mindlessness of it all. I woke up when Jolly came out of the bedroom and barked at me to let her out for her morning run around the backyard.

I realized then that what I had needed to get me moving was the realization that I was going to be very late to work, if I didn't get my ass in gear. Even with my best efforts, I managed to be fifteen minutes late. I parked three cars down from Marie's car. I locked my car, sprinted to the door, and then walked quickly to my office. I nearly slammed into my boss, who was just coming out of the parts office. He was frowning. I suspected I was the reason for this expression.

"I'm sorry, Mr. Watanabe. I had a horrible night last night. Didn't get to sleep until nearly dawn. Then I couldn't wake up when I was supposed to. It won't happen again."

"Ah, Ms. Michaels, I was just taking care of business for you. I'm so sorry to hear about your illness. Are you feeling any better now?"

"Um, yes, a little better now, I think."

"Very good. I left a note on your desk about a phone call you had this morning. Carry on."

I scratched my head in wonder as my boss walked away from me. I wasn't sure how he had concluded that I was sick, but whatever. At least I didn't have to further humiliate myself by telling him that I had fallen asleep next to my cereal bowl. Hopefully I didn't have an imprint on my forehead from the woven placemat I had drooled on during my exhausted nap at the breakfast table.

It was a slow morning, which was fine with me, since I was moving slowly anyway. That half an hour of adrenaline-induced activity had left me feeling even more tired. Even moving slowly, I managed to get caught up on a few things I'd been putting off for weeks. By 10:30, I was caught up enough to make a scouting foray to the water cooler.

Marie was at her desk all right, but she didn't look up when I came into the room. In fact, she studiously avoided looking up the whole time I was in there. It felt as though she were purposefully avoiding acknowledging my presence. I felt hurt, but decided not to say anything for now. Obviously something was seriously wrong, or she'd be her normally cheerful self. The fact that she was trying not to notice me let me know that she knew I was there. I left without saying anything to her.

I positioned my office chair so I could look out through my open door, down the hallway towards the door to Marie's office. I decided that lunchtime was going to be my chance to find out what the hell was going on. It was obvious that something significant had happened between the afternoon she left me that note and the following day when she didn't show up for work. After answering a string of phone calls, I spent a quiet hour arranging and rearranging the contents of my desk drawers while I awaited Marie's departure for lunch.

Finally about 12:30, I heard the door open and saw Marie's small form hurrying down the hallway. I barely had time to grab my jacket and scoot down the hall after her. I caught the door just as it was closing behind her. She kept walking without looking back.

I called her name, but she just kept walking quickly towards her car. I hurried after her and caught her car door before she could shut me out.

"Marie, what is going on?"

She kept her head down and her shades on, even though it was overcast.

"Marie, why are you doing this?"

She didn't look up at me, but she finally sighed deeply. "Jill, please leave me alone. I can't talk right now."

"Okay, but only if you look at me."

"I can't. I'm too ashamed." Her shoulders were shaking, so I guessed that she was crying.

"What is it? What are you ashamed of? Is it the dream? What's wrong?"

She sobbed, "Please, Jill, just leave me alone."

"I won't leave you alone until you tell me why you are ashamed."

I reached in and gently tried to turn her face up towards mine. When she resisted, I let her go. "All right. I'm sorry. I'll leave you alone for now, Marie. But I think you at least owe me an explanation."

She nodded curtly as she shut her car door and started the engine. I walked behind her car towards my own then stopped and waited for Marie to drive past me. I tried to look at her, but she looked away, hiding behind her Ray-Ban anonymity.

I got in my car and headed for home, mostly because I didn't know what else to do with myself. I didn't feel like going to a restaurant to eat, and I hadn't had time to pack a lunch in my mad dash to get to work. I puzzled over what to do as I drove through town. I spotted a car that resembled Marie's in line at the Arby's drive-up window. I pulled in behind it, more out of frustration than anything else. I was surprised when I read the license plate and realized that it was Marie's car after all. There couldn't be two blue Hondas running around Renton with plates that read, "SALSA."

On impulse, I decided to park my car nearby and walk over to hers. She looked shocked to see me and looked in her rearview mirror to see if there was any way to escape. Luck was on my side just then, because another car pulled in close behind hers. I knocked on her window and begged her to let me in. She shook her head. I banged on the window again.

"Come on, Marie. Please let me in. Just for a minute."

Finally I heard her hit the switch that unlocks the doors. I ran to the passenger's side and climbed in.

"Thank you. I promise to keep my hands to myself."

When she made a noise that sounded like a huge hiccup, I realized that she must be crying still.

"God, Marie, what is wrong? Did someone die?"

She shook her head.

"Are you ill?"

"No."

The car ahead moved forward so we inched up as well.

"Is your husband ill?"

A pause then a very quiet "no."

We moved forward again.

"Are you ready to order?"

Marie sat still for a minute then turned towards me, "What did you say?"

"Are you ready to order? You're next in line."

She laughed slightly and shook her head at me. "You're such a funny woman, Jill."

Just then the car in front of us pulled up to the pickup window, which meant that it was our turn to yell at the people inside the little box at the ordering window. After we got our food, we sat in the parking lot and ate in silence, though Marie barely touched her sandwich. After I was finished with my lunch, I decided it was time to broach the subject of the dream from two nights ago.

"So, did you mean what you said the other day about seeing you in my dreams?"

"Jill, please, I don't want to talk about any of that right now. I need to forget all about it. It never happened. We can never talk of this again."

"Why, Marie? What has happened? Why was Enrico so angry when I called? He sounded as though he wanted to kill you and me both. Did you tell him about the dreams?"

"Of course not! How could I?"

"Then what?"

She put her hand over her eyes. "I'm so embarrassed to tell you. It was awful, a terrible mistake. We mustn't talk about the dreams any more."

"So you were there for the second dream. I thought as much, though I wasn't sure. But you said 'dreams,' plural, so you must have been there. What happened? Why mustn't we talk about what happened in our dreams?"

"Because it's over, Jill. Do you hear me? It's over. There will be no more dreams."

"I'm sorry if it scared you, but you shouldn't be ashamed of it. It was beautiful. You have to admit it."

Marie jerked her hand down and turned towards me with anger etched on her face. "I don't have to admit anything to anyone!"

"Ouch! Can I have my head back now?"

"Listen to me, Jill. We mustn't do this any more. We can't eat lunch together. We probably shouldn't even talk to each other."

"Why? Will you just tell me what the hell happened? One minute you're all sexy and seductive, and the next you're snapping at me and acting as though I tried to break up your marriage. What did I do wrong?"

"It wasn't you. It was me."

"Okay, so what did you do?"

"I whispered your name when Enrico was making love to me yesterday morning."

"You what?"

"I think you heard me."

"How? Why?"

"I was still asleep and dreaming. He woke up for some reason and started acting as though he wanted to have sex. I kind of woke up, but was mostly still asleep. When I came, I spoke your name out loud. It was stupid, I know, but I wasn't really quite awake enough to be in control of myself. He caught me by surprise."

"What did he do?"

"He pulled away from me and asked me who the hell Jill was. I didn't know what he was talking about. Then he said, 'You just called out her name while we were fucking. Who the hell is she?' I told him that I didn't know what he was talking about, and that I didn't know anyone named Jill.

"He didn't believe me. He jumped out of bed and starting banging around the house like an elephant with its head stuck inside a garbage can. He was throwing stuff around the living room, breaking things that belong to me. I got out of bed to stop him, but he was so angry and violent that I went back to the bedroom and hid from him. He went on like that for a long time. Perhaps it was only a few minutes, but it felt like hours to me.

"Finally things got quiet. I was afraid to find out what was going on, so I just stayed there, locked in the bedroom. I finally fell asleep and didn't wake up again until my alarm went off. I started towards the bathroom to take a shower, but was so disturbed by the state of the living room, that I went out to find Enrico. He was nowhere to be seen, so I started cleaning up the mess. He had broken every knick-knack I owned, shattered them to bits against the walls. There were glass and ceramic shards all over the room. He even put a crack in one of the front windows.

"I was so scared, Jill. I didn't know what to do. I just kept cleaning up the mess until I heard the car pull into the driveway. Enrico had returned, and he didn't look happy.

He had been drinking. Drinking, Jill, at eight o'clock in the morning! I was terrified of him as soon as I saw his face. Yet I couldn't make myself move. I was paralyzed with fear.

"He came in and didn't say a word to me, at first. When I started getting ready for work, he came in and threw me down on the bed and forced me to have sex with him, even though it would make me late for work. It was disgusting. He was drunk and rough with me. After it was over, I went into the bathroom and vomited. I felt so cheap and abused.

"I've never felt so awful in all my life. While I was in the shower, he stood outside the bathroom door and yelled at me. 'I'll kill her, by God, Marie. I swear I will. If you're having an affair with a woman, I swear to God, I'll kill her!'

"When I got out of the shower, I was too scared to leave the bathroom. I just sat there on the side of my bathtub crying. Finally it was quiet again, so I opened the door. He reached into the gap, grabbed me by my hair, and pulled me into the hallway. He tried to force me to have sex again, only he was too drunk by then to get an erection. So instead he just pawed all over me."

Marie was sobbing again, by this time. I leaned over to touch her on the arm.

"Oh, Jill, it was so disgusting. I was so scared. I didn't know what to do. I wanted to go to work to get away from him, but I couldn't stand the thought of being seen in public. I felt so dirty."

I pulled Marie's head onto my shoulder and held her while she cried. So many emotions were surging through my body; I didn't know which one to address. First there was the rage I felt at Enrico for having terrorized Marie. Then there was the compassion I felt for Marie. On top of that was guilt for having helped to bring the situation into being. Last, and most important, was the love I felt growing inside me for Marie. I wanted to help her and protect her from further harm. She was so small and frightened.

I stroked her hair. "What happened after that, Marie?"

She sat up and tried to wipe her eyes with a tissue. Her sunglasses were in the way, so she lifted them up a little bit in order to staunch the flow of tears washing down her face. That's when I saw the bruise around her right eye. She had tried to cover it with make-up, but her tears had washed a lot of that away.

"My God, Marie, your eye! Did Enrico do that?"

She nodded and starting sobbing again. She removed her sunglasses so I could see the full damage done by Enrico's rage. "He had finally calmed down and fallen asleep. Passed out, I guess. He was out for a couple hours. That's when I called in sick and decided to stay home to keep an eye on him. I was afraid of what else he might do to the house.

"When he awoke, he was a little more sane. I was able to tell him again that I didn't know what he was talking about, and that I wasn't having an affair. I'm sorry I lied and told him that I didn't know anyone named Jill, but I thought it was the only way to convince him that everything was all right. We were able to have a somewhat rational conversation then. We even laughed about it until you called.

"He exploded again after I got off the phone. That's when he struck me and accused me of lying to him. I'm sorry, Jill, but I told him that I hadn't thought about you when he started asking me about women in my life because I could never think about you in such a way. I told him that you were someone from work, but that I didn't even like you."

I patted her hand tenderly. "It's okay, Marie, I understand."

"I didn't want him to go to office and yell at you or worse. I'm so sorry I brought you into all this."

"No, it was my fault. If you hadn't picked up on my attraction to you, none of this would have happened. I'm the one who's sorry."

"Jill, I wasn't completely honest with you the other day. What I didn't tell you was that I was already attracted to you too from the first time I met you. I thought you looked so cute and so butchy. I just wanted to gobble you up."

"Oh yeah?" I smiled at her warmly.

"Yes. But it doesn't matter now. I can't be seen with you. I shouldn't even be here with you now. I can't be sure that Enrico won't start following me around. He's still not convinced that I'm not having an affair. I will have to be very careful from now on." She put her sunglasses back on as though that settled the matter.

"Wait a minute, Marie. You're not going to stay with this guy, are you? Not after he slugged you."

"He's my husband, Jill. It's not like I didn't provoke him. I'm not exactly innocent in all this."

"What? It doesn't matter whether you provoked him. He can't just go around hitting you. He could have seriously injured you."

"It doesn't matter. He's still my husband, and we have to work this out. It will be all right, as long as you and I stop seeing each other. No more lunches after today. No more dreams. I have to forget about you now."

I reached over and pulled her sunglasses gently from your face again. "Marie, you can't let him get away with this. It doesn't matter what is or isn't going on between us. This is just wrong."

"What's wrong, Jill, is for me to be thinking about you in the way I've been thinking about you. I'm a married woman now. I can't do that any more."

"Yes, but—"

"It doesn't matter. It's over now. He won't hit me again, if we end this relationship before anything else happens. I will just have to get over it and so will you. We'll have to pretend it never happened."

"That will be awfully hard to do after that second dream." There was a few seconds of silence as I replayed the dream in my head. I suspect Marie was doing the same thing. I felt a surge of electric energy run through my body. When I looked into Marie's eyes again, I could tell she must've felt it too. Neither of us said anything.

I leaned towards her to kiss her. She closed her eyes, but put out a hand to stop me. "No, this mustn't get any more complicated. We must stop it before it starts. Because if it starts, Jill, I won't want it to stop."

I stopped my forward progression and looked into her eyes, hoping to find the passion I saw in my dreams. All I saw was fear and despair.

"Okay, Marie. As you wish. I'll leave you alone."

I turned to get out of the car, but felt her small, soft hand on my arm stopping me. "Thank you for understanding, Jill. I'm sorry."

"Oh, I don't understand it, Marie. It makes no sense at all to me. I'm simply respecting your decision. Nothing more. I can't even begin to comprehend why you would want to stay with Enrico after what he did to you. It makes my blood boil. And believe me, if he ever does it again, I will personally call the police and report it, after I've taken you to a place of safety. Do you hear me, Marie? He won't be allowed to do this to you ever again."

The calm tone of my voice was in complete contrast to the rage I was experiencing inside. I amazed even myself. I had never felt so totally in control of myself as I did in that moment. I knew without a doubt that I would follow through with swift action if the man ever even attempted any act of violence towards her again.

I put my hand over Marie's. "Please don't make it any harder than it already is. Your touch ignites my body and soul. If we can't be lovers, even dream lovers, then please don't touch me like that. It feels too much like torture."

She pulled her hand free of my light grasp. "I'm sorry. I wish things could be different."

"They could be different, but I'm not the one to make that decision. It's up to you and you alone. Goodbye, Marie."

Chapter 5
Out of my Dreams

I walked back over to my car and opened the door. The clock on the dashboard let me know that it was nearly time to return to work. I turned and watched as Marie drove away, presumably out of my life, certainly out of my dreams. The thought of working with her, yet not talking to her, made me feel hollow inside. Before all this happened, I had really enjoyed our social exchanges. My feelings for her made it easy to go to work every day. I knew I would see her at least once. I hadn't realized how much I had come to take her presence in my life for granted, however brief our encounters.

I had grown comfortable with the situation as it had been. Marie, although completely inaccessible romantically, was like a ray of sunshine filtering through these otherwise gray and bleak days. I wasn't sure I wanted to continue to work so near her and yet be estranged from her. I cursed myself for having let it get out of hand. Then I smiled as I realized that Marie had been the one pursuing me. I had been content merely to nibble on the crumbs that dropped from the bread that nourished her.

For me, she was like a fragrant rose growing in a neighbor's garden. She may not have been mine, but at least I was allowed to enjoy the scent of her flowering as it wafted on the breeze. Only now it felt as though someone had come and chopped down the entire plant, leaving me to watch the fallen petals as they shriveled up and died beneath my feet.

Somehow it just didn't feel right. Marie had always seemed so full of life and love. How could she surrender that beautiful soul to a man of violence? It wasn't as though I felt that she should be mine. I just knew that she shouldn't be his. I wanted so badly to see her stand up for herself. It hurt to see her cowering to his angry, masculine strength. I knew it wouldn't be long before he destroyed her, emotionally, if not physically. I was a witness to the damage he had already inflicted, and even if he never laid another hand on her, the threat of violence would be there just below the surface.

As I drove back to work, I tried to think of ways to help her. I decided to give an old college friend of mine a call. She had been a psychology major, who had gone on to graduate school and become a social worker. Maybe she would have some answers to Marie's problems. At least she could provide a sympathetic ear for my woes. She had always been good at that. I consoled myself with this thought, as I drove into the parking lot at work.

I noticed that Marie was still sitting in her car. She was reapplying the make-up she had smudged and smeared with all her crying. I walked by her car without even a backward glance. Yet the knife in my heart twisted and turned with each step. I wanted so badly to run to her and carry her away with me to some place unknown, to some place where we would both be safe from the violence of this world.

I shut my office door behind me, hoping that I wouldn't be disturbed for the rest of the day. I had just sat down at my desk when the phone rang. I picked it up in one swift motion. "Parts department, this is Jill."

The voice on the other end of the line said, "Jill, huh? What's your last name, Jill?"

"Um, actually, I'd say that was irrelevant. More to the point, what can I do for you today?" I said as cheerfully as I could muster in my present gloomy mood.

"That all depends."

The voice on the line sounded suspiciously like Enrico. A shot of adrenaline rushed through my body. "Sir, did you need a part for your car, or should I direct your call to another department?"

"Yeah, I need a part, but not for my car. I need the part of Marie that you stole from me."

"What on earth are you talking about?" My mind raced through possible options. If I hung up, would he think I was feeling guilty about Marie? If I talked to him, I might learn something that could help Marie. I opted to try the latter, since I had the safety of the phone between us.

"You know what I'm talking about. I came in this morning to see for myself what you looked like. You're obviously a dyke, and I want you to leave Marie alone."

"I have no idea what you're talking about. Good day!"

I hung the phone up then began pacing around the office. I had noticed a man looking into my office through the parts window this morning. I had asked him if he needed help, but he just shook his head and quickly walked away. I hadn't thought anything about it at the time. I decided that I would have to tell Marie about this, but I didn't want to talk to her in public. I had my doubts as to whether I could lure her into the women's restroom for a *tête-à-tête*, so I picked up the phone and dialed her direct line.

"Good afternoon, service department, Marie speaking."

I loved to hear the slight rolling of the "r" in Marie. Although her Latino accent was faint most of the time, it was more noticeable when she pronounced her own name.

"Marie?   This is Jill.   Please don't hang up.   I have something very important to tell you."

"Yes, what is it?"

"It's about Enrico. He just called me. He didn't identify himself, but a man just phoned me to tell me that he had come in this morning to get a look at me. He said that he could tell that I was a dyke."

"I see. What else did he say?"

"When I asked him if he needed a part for his car, he told me that he needed a part, but not for his car. He wanted the part of you that I stole from him."

"Jesus, Joseph, and Mary! What did you say to that?"

"I told him that I had no idea what he was talking about, and then I hung up. I didn't know what else to do."

"I will bring that paperwork right away. Thank you for calling. I will be there in just a moment."

"What? Oh, yeah, okay. I'll be waiting."

I placed the receiver back in its cradle and sat for a moment with my head in my hands. A few minutes later there was a light knock at the door. Marie stuck her head into the office.

"May I come in?"

"Of course. Sit down," I rose and gestured to my chair.

Marie sat down quickly and turned to look up at me as I began pacing the floor.

"This is not good, Jill. This is a very bad sign. If Enrico has seen you and can tell that you are lesbian, then I'm afraid it's all over. I don't even want to go home. He will kill me."

"Does he know about your past?"

"Yes, of course he does. We first became friends right after my girlfriend in college dumped me. His girlfriend had just dumped him too. We met in the bar where all the college students hung out. We were both depressed and had been drinking. We started talking and pouring out our life history to each other. It was rather pathetic at the time and yet strangely comforting too. We were like two college buddies discussing our woman troubles. By the end of the night, we were roaring drunk.

"The bartender finally kicked us out. We decided to go to his apartment so we could keep talking and drinking. We wound up having sex, I think. I don't remember much of that night. We were both horribly hung over the next day. Neither of us wanted to move. Later on when we had recovered some, we started talking and laughing again. Then we ended up having sex again. I kept telling myself that I was just consoling myself for Theresa's awful treatment of me. I figured that when I left his apartment I'd never see him again. I didn't even give him my phone number.

"Somehow he tracked me down and showed up at my door. I agreed to have dinner with him, still thinking it was just a temporary fling. I never dreamed I would end up marrying the man."

"So why did you?"

"I don't know, Jill. I came to care for him. He is very handsome and an energetic lover. It felt good to have someone who desired me. At the time, I was feeling pretty low and very undesirable. I don't know. It just happened.

"It didn't hurt that my mother fell in love with him when she first met him. Of course, she probably would've fallen in love with any man I brought home. She refused to accept my attraction to women. She found fault with every woman I dated. I finally stopped trying to get her to accept them or me and realized that as long as I had a female lover, my mother didn't want me around. She was ashamed of me.

"Once she decided that Enrico was to be her future son-in-law, it was very difficult to stop that snowball from rolling downhill and gaining momentum. Mama is a very dominant force in our family. Papa just goes along with most of what she says. Very seldom does he speak up about anything. I don't know what he thought of Enrico. Oddly enough, he didn't seem to mind that I dated women. Perhaps it was okay with him because it meant that he didn't have to worry about some punk getting his youngest daughter pregnant. That's what happened to my older sister. That was the family scandal that really seemed to break Papa's heart. He was never the same after that. I suppose he felt as though he had failed to protect her somehow.

"She has three children now and no husband. The guy who got her pregnant agreed to marry her, but they kept putting it off for one reason or another. Finally he took off after the third pregnancy was announced. She works very hard, but she still can't make ends meet. Papa has to give her money for groceries every month.

"In spite of all that, Mama still wanted me to find a man to marry. That's all she talked about when I went home to visit. When I brought Enrico home for dinner one night, she thought that I had finally been rescued from my sinful lesbian lifestyle. I decided to go along with it for a while, just to get her to stop talking about it. Unfortunately it took my getting married to Enrico to get her to shut up about it."

"So you married Enrico for your mother?'

"Not exactly. I really cared for him. It's just that it was easier to go along with Mama's dreams than to try to rebuild the dreams I had for myself before Theresa dumped me."

"Why did Theresa leave you? I can't imagine why anyone would walk away from you, Marie."

She smiled indulgently. "Jill, you don't really know me."

"Perhaps not, but you're a goddess to me."

She blushed when I said this then stood as if to leave. "You are so sweet, Jill, but I need to figure out what I'm going to do now. I'm afraid to go home."

"Where do your parents live?"

"Yakima, but I can't go there. My mother would side with Enrico for one thing. For another thing, I wouldn't be able to go to work from there. The drive would be too much for me every day. Perhaps on the weekends I can stay there."

"You're welcome to stay at my house, though I suppose you wouldn't want to do that."

"Right now I don't know what I want."

"Do you have a lawyer?"

"No. I haven't needed one."

"Well, you should probably talk to someone about pressing charges against him for hitting you so you can get a restraining order placed on him. That way he can't come after you at work or anywhere else."

"Maybe I should just call to see if it was really him. Perhaps it was a prankster."

"Marie, a prankster wouldn't know what I look like, and he wouldn't know you by name. It was Enrico, all right."

"Yes, but we haven't done anything wrong. Maybe I can get him to believe that."

"Marie, we may not have done anything in real life, but we made love in our dreams. Then you called out my name while you were in the throes of sexual passion with him. How are you ever going to explain that without him getting pissed again?"

"Oh God, Jill, I hate this. Our marriage may not have been perfect, but it was comfortable. I felt secure and happy for the most part, although I hadn't stopped being attracted to women just because I was married. If anything, women began to be even more appealing. I may have had the approval of my mother, but I missed the loving ways of a woman. That's why I was so pleased when I met you. I knew right away that you were lesbian. I could feel that dynamic dance of sexual energy between us.

"I was content, however, to let it remain unspoken. That is, at least, until I had that first dream about you. Then it was so exciting emotionally and sexually that I could hardly contain myself. I guess I wanted to have my world with

Enrico by day, while enjoying my dream world with you by night. Perhaps I'm being punished for my greed."

She bowed her head and began to cry softly. I leaned down and put my hands lightly on either side of her shoulders. "You're not being punished for your sins, Marie. You didn't commit any."

"But I did, Jill, in my heart."

I cupped her chin in my hand and lifted her face to mine. "Thank you for those dreams. They are some of the best moments of my life. Especially the second one. I've never felt as totally possessed by anyone as I did that night you took me on the couch. Real life sex has never been that potent."

She smiled a sad smile and wiped her tears again. "I know. Me too." She sniffed then stood up. "I need to get back to my office."

"No, Marie, we need to get you to a lawyer before the day is out. Let me find Mr. Watanabe and explain enough of this to him to gain his sympathy. He's a good man, even if he is a little out of it sometimes."

"But what will you tell him?"

"No more than I have to. Go back to your office and wrap things up for the day. I'm going to call a friend of mine. She's a social worker, and she may be able to help us."

"Okay, Jill. Thank you. I feel so powerless in all this. I don't know what I would do without you."

"Yeah, well, I feel partly responsible for all this."

"No, Jill, you are not to blame. I am the one who started this business with the dream. I told you it was prophetic."

I smiled, trying to contain the hope that was leaping up from my heart. "Oh, yeah? Well, we'll see. First we need to get you some help."

I shut the door behind her then sat down at my desk to thumb through my Rolodex for Linda's cell phone number. I got her voice mail, so I left a brief message explaining the urgency of the call. Then I went in search of my boss. I found him on the sales floor talking with some of the sales people. When he was finished talking with them, I approached him.

"Excuse me, Mr. Watanabe?"

"Yes, Ms. Michaels?"

"Sir, could I speak to you in private for a moment?"

"Why certainly. Come into my office."

We stepped into his comfortable office. He offered me a chair across from his desk. He waited for me to be seated before sitting down. I briefly outlined the trouble between Enrico and Marie without getting into an explanation about our relationship and the dreams. I merely brought out the need for Marie's safety from her violent and estranged husband. I requested the last couple hours of the afternoon off for both of us, so I could escort her to a lawyer. Mr. Watanabe granted my request, remarking that one of his four daughters had married a man with a violent temper. She managed to get a divorce from him, but not without considerable trouble and expense. He wished us luck and asked to be kept apprised of Marie's situation. I left his office feeling relieved. I wasn't sure what he would think of my role in all this, but he didn't act as though anything was amiss.

When I got back to my office, I checked my voice mail for messages then set everything in order on my desk for whoever was going to have to fill in for me. Just as I was putting on my jacket, the phone rang. I picked it up and was encouraged to hear Linda's concerned voice on the line.

"Yes, love, bring her around as soon as you can. I can squeeze her in this afternoon between appointments."

I thanked Linda, as well as any deities who might be listening, for making this as simple as possible. Then I scooted over to Marie's office to collect her, smiling warmly at Candace, who was frowning while Marie gathered her belongings to leave. Apparently she was not happy about having to cover for Marie again. Such is life. I knew for a fact that Marie had covered for Candace many times, whereas Marie had never missed a day of work up until yesterday.

When Marie was ready, we headed out the door, agreeing on the need to take both cars. She didn't want to leave her car in the parking lot, just in case Enrico decided to come looking for her. I gave her the directions to Linda's office in the event that we got separated in traffic. Then we headed for Bellevue.

Chapter 6
A Friend Indeed

We were ahead of most of the commuter traffic, so the trip to Bellevue was fairly quick. Marie arrived at Linda's office building right behind me. Together we walked upstairs to her second-floor waiting room. After a few years as a state social worker, Linda had opened her own counseling service, offering help to women and children in trouble. She shared an office building with several lawyers, with whom she frequently shared clients.

I led the way down the hallway to Linda's office. The receptionist, a young woman of about twenty, greeted us. She asked us to be seated. Linda was still in a meeting with another client. We made ourselves as comfortable as possible on the sofa.

It was apparent that Marie was very nervous. She kept picking up different magazines from the coffee table, flipping through them quickly then replacing each one with another. It was obvious that nothing was actually making an impression on her mind. It looked merely like something to do with her hands, which were trembling slightly.

After the fourth speedy magazine perusal, I reached out and put my hand on her arm. "It's going to all right, Marie. Linda knows a lot of people, including scores of lawyers, police officers, and court officials. You will be in good hands with her and her colleagues."

Marie smiled timidly in my direction. "It's not your friend I'm worried about. It's Enrico. He's already destroyed a lot of my belongings. There's no telling what he'll do next. If I don't come home tonight, and I don't call him, he'll come looking for me. He already found out who you are. It won't take him long to find out where you live. He tracked me down years ago after that first night I spent with him. He's very charming when he wants to be. He'll manage to get your address somehow."

"It's okay, Marie. I've got a dog and a good set of locks on my doors. Plus I have a cell phone, in addition to my regular phone line. I can call the police at a moment's notice."

Just then the door opened and a tall, distinguished, blonde came out smiling, arms outstretched. "Jill, it's so good to see you again. It's been too long, you know. It's not as though we live light years away from one another." She gave me a hug and a kiss on the cheek then turned her attention towards Marie.

Linda is one of those people who can make everyone she talks to feel as though they are the most important person in the world. I stepped back as I watched Linda administer emotional first aid to Marie's soul. Marie's sensitivity to psychic undercurrents was surely picking up the deep human warmth that was flowing through Linda. Marie's demeanor visibly changed under the influence of this wonderful woman. You could see her starting to relax a little bit.

"Now usually, Marie, I confer with my clients alone, unless they specifically request someone else's presence in the room. That means that Miss Jill here will have to cool her heels until we're through chatting. Is that all right with you, or would you prefer the moral support?"

"I think I would feel better talking to you alone. I really don't want to drag Jill into this any more than necessary."

"So be it." She smiled in my direction. You heard the lady, Jill. Be a doll and get lost for about an hour."

"Aye, aye, captain!" I saluted Linda, smiled warmly at Marie, and did an about face to head for parts unknown. Once outside Linda's office, I began to feel the weight of Marie's burden slipping away. I trusted Linda to take good care of Marie. That was enough for the time being. Now I just had to figure out how to kill an hour's time without getting back out into the evening commuter traffic.

I sat in my car for a few minutes, weighing my options. I finally decided to try taking a nap. I had been so wired from everything that had happened today that I had almost forgotten how tired I was from not sleeping well last night. Having placed Marie in competent hands, I felt relieved enough to experience all the fatigue I had been pushing aside in order to make it through the day.

When a blast from someone's car horn woke me, I checked my watch and realized that I had been asleep for over an hour. I jumped out of my car and raced upstairs to Linda's office. I needn't have hurried, however, as the pair were still conferring. The receptionist, whose name was Tillie, offered me some coffee and cookies, which I declined. Then she offered me some water, which I graciously accepted. I gulped it down quickly, since I was suddenly feeling parched.

I started thumbing through magazines, trying to find something interesting to read. I asked Tillie where the restroom was then set off to find relief from the pressure on my bladder. The water I just drank wasn't helping that situation. On my way back, I nearly ran into Linda and Marie, who were finally coming out of Linda's inner office. Marie was smiling, though it was apparent she had done a good deal of crying in the past hour.

Linda handed Marie her business card. "Here's my card. It has both my home and office numbers. I have voice mail on both lines, and I check it frequently. Have you decided where to stay tonight?"

Marie bowed her head. "Not really. I don't want to go to my family's house because I won't be able to go to work tomorrow."

"Well, here's the address and phone number of a woman's shelter, if you need it."

I didn't wish to interrupt them, but I thought it was important to reiterate to Marie that my house was still an option. "You're welcome to stay at my place, Marie, if you want to. I have a spare bedroom for guests. It wouldn't take long for me to clear a space for your belongings. It's up to you. If you wouldn't feel comfortable, then I understand."

"I guess it would be all right, though I worry about Enrico finding out where you live. Perhaps it would be safe enough for one night. Then I could make other arrangements tomorrow. I really don't want to put you in harm's way, Jill. You've been so kind to me, and I appreciate it very much."

"No problem, Marie. I'm glad I can help."

At this point Linda interjected, "Marie, you mentioned wanting to use the ladies' room. Tillie can show you where that is, while I catch up with my long lost friend for the briefest of moments."

While Tillie and Marie headed towards the restroom, Linda ushered me into her office. "I don't wish to alarm you, Jill, but this sounds serious. I don't know how much Marie has told you about her Romeo, and obviously I can't divulge anything she said to me that she hasn't already told you. However I will tell you that I'm going to have a friend keeping an eye on you two for a while. He's a good friend of mine, and he owes me a few favors. I'm about to cash them all in on this case. Marie is in real danger and so are you. Watch yourself and don't try to be a hero."

"Um, okay, whatever you say. Who should I watch out for, so I know which are the bad guys and the good guys?"

"Last I knew, Mack had a silver Crown Victoria, fairly new. He may be in one of several vehicles though so as not to be too obvious."

She reached into her desk drawer and pulled out a photograph of a man, who looked to be in his early forties, with blond hair and bulging muscles. He looked like a lifeguard turned body builder.

"This is Vincent McElroy, though nearly everyone calls him Mack."

"Probably because he looks like a truck."

"Which is why he is the perfect retired cop for this job."

"Linda, I can't afford to hire a bodyguard."

"You don't have to, Jill, and neither does Marie. Like I said, he owes me many favors. He's on my time."

"Thanks, Linda. As ever, you are a gem beyond compare."

"You flatter me, Jill, but I'll take all the positive feedback I can get. It's not always abundant in a field like mine. Still I wouldn't want to be doing anything else."

"Thanks for everything, Linda."

"My pleasure, love. Make sure she gets to her appointment with the lawyer tomorrow. She needs to move quickly before Enrico tracks her down.

I nodded.

Linda reached out and touched my shoulder. "One more thing, Jill. Think long and hard before you get romantically involved with Marie. She told me about your shared dreams. Be very careful. She's a very sensitive woman, and she's vulnerable now. Tiptoe around her heart. One false step right now could crush her and send her back into Enrico's violent world. That's the last thing she needs. She fell for him on the rebound after the devastation of one broken relationship. She doesn't need to repeat that history.

"Still, Marie is a strong-willed individual. She had to be in order to come out as bisexual while she was in college. That had to have been a difficult decision. Her familial relationships suffered for that decision, and it took the loss of the woman she loved to turn her back into what she perceived to be a dutiful daughter. She has the inner strength to survive this ordeal, but it isn't going to be easy for you or her."

I pondered her words while she caught her breath and scrutinized me. "You're already in love with her, aren't you?"

I nodded pensively. She placed her hand on my back. "Oh, Jill, you always were a sucker for a beautiful soul. You chose well. It won't be easy, if it's to be at all. Good luck to you both. Call me if you need me for anything. I love you, sweetheart. Now get out there before we make Marie paranoid."

Linda followed me out the door. "Call me once in a while, love. I do miss talking with you. You were my one sane friend those last couple of years in college. You probably still are my only sane friend in the world. Don't let's be strangers. I need your wonderful heart and loving eyes to help keep me on track."

She gave me another big hug before I left. She gave Marie one too. "Now do keep me posted. I want to know that you are both safe. And please, don't hesitate to call me in an emergency situation. My phone is always on the hook for either of you."

Marie responded with warmth, "Thank you so much, Linda, for everything. I have much to think about, but you've helped me to get it all sorted in my head. I'll be in touch."

I blew Linda a kiss and nodded at Tillie on our way out.

As soon as we were in the hallway, Marie startled me by asking, "Were you two lovers in college?"

"Linda?" I shook my head sternly. "God, no. She's strictly heterosexual, as far as I've ever known. Though she isn't married at the moment. She married young then got divorced before she ever went to college. It was a nasty divorce too, as she tells it. I think that experience is partly why she chose to go into social work and definitely why she decided to come to the states. In case her accent didn't give her away, she's from England. It's also part of the reason why she chose to focus her work on women and children in difficult situations.

"I suspect that she thinks of me as a younger sister. I know I felt as though she often played the role of an older sister for me. I don't have any sisters, so she became my surrogate in college. Even though we don't see each other frequently, we try to stay in touch as much we can."

We started walking slowly down the stairs to our cars.

"Do you have any brothers?" Marie asked.

"Yep, two younger and one older. It was easy to be a tomboy around those three. We used to make up the most awesome football foursome in our neighborhood. That was back when people actually knew their neighbors. I can't say that I know many of the people who live around me now. It's a shame really. What about you? Do you have any siblings?"

"I have one older sister. That's the one who got pregnant in high school. I also have three older brothers. I'm rather worried about them. When they hear that Enrico struck me, I fear that they will retaliate. They are very protective of both their sisters. I suspect that's why my sister's boyfriend vanished completely. He knows my brothers and must've known that staying in the same town with them was not an option once he dumped their sister."

"So your brothers are in Yakima then?"

"Two live in Yakima near my parents. One moved to San Antonio, Texas last year, though my father said that he may be moving back soon."

"Well, they could come in handy. Three brothers against Enrico could be just what we need to turn the tables."

"No, Jill, I really don't want to get them involved. I don't want anyone else I love embroiled in my mess."

I noted that she had said "anyone *else* that she loved." I hoped that she was implying that I was the one she loved who was already involved. Then again, she could have been referring to Enrico.

When we got to our cars, I jotted down my address then told her to try to stay behind me if possible. The route to my house is a rather circuitous one. I really didn't want us to get separated on the trip there, especially since I didn't know whether Enrico might be waiting for us. Hopefully we had gotten an early enough jump on him. He would only now be expecting Marie to be on the way home. I didn't want to take any chances though. So far our luck was holding out.

Chapter 7
Tending Home Fires

As we neared my house, I began checking for strange cars. Nothing looked amiss, so I pulled up in front of my house then motioned for Marie to pull up under the carport. I pulled in behind her, figuring that my car would block the view of hers for the most part. Just to be safe, I asked Marie if she would mind if I threw a tarp over her car. She didn't, so I fetched one while she got out of the car and waited for me. She stood there looking around nervously while I did the work of hiding her vehicle from sight.

I led her to the front door and unlocked it. Jolly jumped on me before I could even get in the door. "How ya doing, girl? Did you miss me? Of course you did, and I missed you too." I patted her head and dodged her spongy dog tongue.

Marie smiled at Jolly's affectionate welcome. "This is your watchdog?"

"Hey now, I said that I had a dog and a good set of locks. I never said anything about having a watchdog. Still, she does bark when anyone comes to the door or gets near the house. So I guess she really is a watchdog. She's just a really friendly one. She'd be more likely to lick a prowler to death than bite him. But at least she would let me know if someone is on the premises.

After Jolly had calmed down a little bit, I said, "I have a T-shirt you can sleep in tonight. We might need to go to the drugstore and pick up a toothbrush. I don't think I have a spare at the moment."

"Actually, Jill, I keep a little toiletry kit in my purse for emergencies."

"Really?" I smirked at her.

"I know it seems weird, but mostly I use it at work after lunch to clean my teeth."

"Whoa, how very hygienic of you."

"My father's a dentist. What can I say?" She smiled at me a little nervously.

"Are you interested in dinner?"

"I guess, though I can't say that I have much of an appetite right now. My nerves are wound so tight I don't know if I can digest anything. What did you have in mind?"

"Hmm, let's go see what our options are." I walked into the kitchen and started rummaging in the refrigerator. I didn't see anything of particular interest, so I checked the freezer. Not much there either. Finally I found a box of pasta and a jar of spaghetti sauce in the pantry. Marie, who had wandered into the kitchen behind me, nodded at my find, so I set myself to the task of cooking it for us.

"I'm sorry I don't have much to offer. I need to go to the grocery store, but I was waiting for my next paycheck."

"It's okay, Jill. Spaghetti will be fine. I really hate to impose on you like this."

"Nonsense! I'm delighted to have company."

I motioned for Marie to sit down at the kitchen table while I worked. I nearly tripped over Jolly while I was moving around the kitchen preparing dinner, so I told her to lie down or go outside. She opted to lie down at Marie's feet and offer her irresistible belly for scratching. Marie leaned over her and rubbed and scratched until Jolly's leg started twitching. Marie started laughing. "You are so funny, Jolly. Your name suits you well. You make even me feel jolly when I play with you."

Jolly responded by squirming and writhing on the floor with her eyes rolled back in her head. Marie laughed again.

I looked down at my clownish companion, "Jolly, you're making a spectacle of yourself."

Marie smiled up at me. "And I'm loving every minute of it. She's so cute, Jill. It makes me miss having a dog."

"You don't have any pets?"

"No, Enrico doesn't like animals. My family always had animals underfoot. Usually a dog or two and several cats wandering around outside." She paused for a moment. "You know, Jill, I really should call Enrico. He will be worried, which will only make him more upset and angry."

I hesitated. "Okay, but what are you going to tell him?"

"I'll tell him I'm going to stay with a friend because I don't want to be around him while he's angry. I won't tell him who or where."

"What did Linda say about contacting him?"

"She said that I could probably make phone contact but refuse to meet with him until I've spoken to the lawyer whose name she gave me."

"How do you think he'll respond to that?"

"I don't know, Jill. I've never seen him so angry. I'm hoping that he's calmed down some by now."

"How long have you two been married?"

"Not quite two years. We've had our share of quarrels, but nothing like this. Certainly nothing to make me suspect he'd ever strike me. I've never thought of him as being particularly violent or anything. I've seen him get angry when he's working on his cars and something doesn't go right. But I just figured that was frustration."

"What do you mean?"

"If he got angry about a part that wouldn't do what he wanted it do, he sometimes took a wrench to it and hit it a few times in frustration. I just viewed that as a guy thing."

"How long did you two know each other before you got married?"

"About three months."

"When did you decide to marry him?"

"He asked me the first month we were together, but I told him there was no way I could marry him before he met my family. So we went to see my parents the following weekend. My mother, of course, fell in love with him instantly."

"Because he was a man?"

"Well, yes, and a handsome one at that."

"Hmm."

"What are you thinking, Jill?"

"I don't know. That just doesn't seem like a very long engagement."

"Yeah, like lesbians have long courtships before they move in together."

"Ah, good point. Still, to marry a man you hardly know. I mean, with lesbians you know you can always move out. There are few legal entanglements, at least not usually."

"Unless you are Martina Navratilova or someone equally famous."

"Yeah, exactly."

"Jill, you know what?"

"What?"

"I think you are prejudiced against men."

My brows furrowed in response. "Why on earth would you say that?"

"Because you know perfectly well that lesbians move in with each other based only on an immediate attraction, yet you don't seem to be willing to make the same allowance for heterosexual couples."

"Okay, but wouldn't that make me prejudiced against heterosexual couples, rather than just men? At any rate, I can't say that I've ever had reason to consider the issue before. It's food for thought. And speaking of food, I think I hear the water boiling."

As I went over to the stove to check the water, I thought about what Marie said and concluded that there was probably some truth to it. I concluded that heterosexuals have as much right as lesbians to make life-changing decisions based on the initial heat of sexual attraction. Not that it was a particularly good way to run your life, but such is the way of the world.

After I started the pasta cooking, I turned to Marie. "The choice is yours whether to call Enrico. The phone is on the end table in the living room. Help yourself. I'll stay in here and mind the hearth, so you can have some privacy."

"Thank you for understanding, Jill."

Marie left the kitchen, and I was left to wonder why I couldn't have been the one Marie met on the rebound. At least I would never have hit her. On the contrary, I could easily find myself worshipping that woman. Hell, I already had worshipped her in my dreams.

The reminder of my dreams made me desire Marie all over again. It was very hard, however, to juxtapose the Marie I was acquainted with at work with the woman I knew in my dreams. I realized they were one and the same, but having sex in your dreams is one thing. While the aftertaste lingers in your mind and body, there's no getting around the social habits and obstacles that stand between us during the day. The dreams were more like a shared fantasy. However titillating they may have been, they were still just that— fantasies with no basis in reality.

In the waking world there had been an undercurrent between us. But everything that happened in the daytime was implied and unspoken, and therefore subject to loads of misinterpretation. Nothing had ever been said that would lead me to think that she could ever love me. All I had were teasing innuendoes and the memory of those hot, sexy dreams. We still hadn't actually talked about the second dream, so I couldn't even be sure that they were identical. What if her dreams had started with me making love to her, but ended with Enrico? *But no, she called out my name, not his. God, this is all so confusing.*

I checked the pasta to see if it was done, more out of a need to be doing something than the thought that it could actually be ready. It wasn't ready, so I sat down and started playing with Jolly. She had curled up under the table, but she perked up when I sat down on the floor next to her.

"You're a good dog, Jolly." She rolled over to allow me access to that insatiable tummy of hers. I rubbed her down good then she sat up to lick me on the face. About that time, I heard Marie raise her voice on the phone. Then I heard a string of Spanish I couldn't begin to translate fast enough, even after several years of Spanish classes in high school. It sounded harsh, though, whatever she was saying. I fought back the desire to go out and check on her. To occupy my time, I got off the floor, washed my hands, and then started setting the table for dinner.

By the time I had finished, things had gotten very quiet, so I ventured out to check on her. Marie was sitting on the couch looking somewhat shell-shocked. The telephone handset was back on its charger.

"Are you okay?"

Marie nodded then bowed her head and started sobbing. I rushed to her side and put my arm around her small, shaking frame.

"What did he say, Marie?"

Marie shook her head and continued sobbing. I sat there quietly waiting until her tears subsided. She leaned into my embrace and just stayed there for several minutes. I let her take her time composing herself. I certainly wasn't going to hurry her up. Not when I could enjoy the feeling of holding her close to me. I inhaled the scent of her hair. The fragrance of it seemed distinctly familiar to me, one I recognized from my dreams.

After several blissful minutes, she tilted her head back and looked up at me. I saw pleading in her eyes. I wasn't quite sure what to do in that moment. I didn't want to move in on her while she was experiencing such anguish over her husband. That didn't seem right somehow. Yet she just kept looking up at me as though she wanted me to kiss her.

Finally I whispered, "If you keep looking at me like that, I'm going to have to kiss you."

She closed her eyes for a moment then opened them again. This time there was a tiny flame in them. Unable to resist the attraction of her eyes, I bent over her to kiss her. Before my mouth could reach hers, she extended a hand towards me and cupped my cheek in it. Then she lightly brushed my lips with her thumb, tracing a path around my mouth until I allowed my lips to part for her. The tip of my tongue caressed her thumb then drew it into my mouth. I released it again and began to tease the palm of her hand with my tongue, allowing it to flicker between each of her fingers. I could sense the heat of her passion rising to meet mine.

I followed the path of her arm with my mouth, alternately kissing and nibbling my way towards her lips. Finally when my face was so close to hers I could feel her breath on it, I brought my lips to a gentle landing upon hers. She returned my kiss with soft and supple lips. At first our kisses were sweet and tender. Then they became enflamed with consuming passion, our tongues wrestling with the weight of the sensuality of each other. When our lips finally parted company, I felt completely breathless. My heart felt as though it had been set adrift on a sea of tranquil waters. Yet I knew that floating aimlessly on the sea, with no rudder or sail, could be a dangerous activity.

After allowing myself to float for a few more seconds, I finally said in a voice that was husky with desire, "You know, we really shouldn't be doing this."

She looked up at me through the haze of sexual fire. "Is that so?" she whispered.

I nodded. "There's nothing I would like more than to scoop you up in my arms and carry you to bed with me. But the fact remains that you are married. We can't afford to do something we might both regret later."

Marie smiled up at me and nodded, but didn't attempt to remove herself from my embrace.

"I'm serious. What we're doing here could have serious repercussions."

Marie nodded again.

"You don't want to stop, do you?"

Marie shook her head slowly then she reached up a hand and pulled my face down towards hers again. What can I say? I'm human. I kissed her again with all the pent-up passion that had been boiling inside me all these months I had been attracted to this beautiful co-worker of mine. I felt her hands slide down to my shirt and begin to unbutton it. I pulled away from her and opened my eyes.

"Are you absolutely certain you want to do this?"

She nodded again and kept unbuttoning until my shirt fell slack and my breasts hung through the gaping lapels. She began massaging them. Then she leaned up and began to nibble them until they were hard with excitement.

"I want you, Jill," she whispered in a soft voice. "It has been far too long since I've been with a woman."

I closed my eyes and allowed the rush of sexual energy to course through my veins. "Yes, but, doesn't this qualify as adultery?"

"Jill, I'm married, not dead. Women in ancient cultures were never forced to limit themselves to one sexual partner. Surely you've read enough feminist literature to know that."

She continued, quite persuasively, to caress my body with her hands and lips.

I struggled to keep my wits about me, but it was getting increasingly difficult with all that persuasion going on. "Yes, I know all that," I said between kisses, "but our society is different."

"Our society is stifling. Passion is wonderful, and passion is what I want to experience with you. Right now."

She pushed me up and away from her then directed me down until my back was on the seat of the sofa. With deft fingers, she undid my jeans and pulled open the fly. Then, as though she'd had another idea, she stood up and began to unbutton her own blouse slowly, glancing at me periodically to make sure I was watching. Not that there was anything I could do to stop myself from enjoying the show.

Once all the buttons were open, she just stood there, allowing my eyes to explore the luscious brown skin that was peeking through the opening of her top. Then she smiled at me, turned around, and struck the same pose she had taken in that last dream. I sat upright suddenly. "So you were there!"

"Of course, I was. Why do you think I called out your name in the dark?"

She let her top fall to the floor and lifted up her hair, letting it fall slowly back down again. Remembering my role in this drama, I managed to slither off the couch and crawl on my hands and knees towards Marie. She turned around and allowed me access to her beautiful breasts with their chocolate nipple toppings. I licked them slowly, savoring the taste of Marie's skin.

"God, I love you, Marie," I managed to say in between gulping bites.

"Jill, didn't your mother ever teach you not to talk with your mouth full?"

I snickered softly then stuffed my mouth even more. This brought on a moan from Marie. She reached around and unzipped her skirt. I leaned back as she peeled skirt, pantyhose, and underwear down to the floor. She slipped her feet out of her shoes and flung the cumbersome apparel aside. Then she stood up again so I could resume my task of dream re-enactment. While it wasn't accurate frame by frame, it was undoubtedly real. There would be no alarms to awaken me from this wet dream.

As I made love to her, Marie ran her hands through my hair, causing it to stand up in short spikes. When her passion had been slaked somewhat, she pulled back and laughed at her own handiwork.

"I think I like the punk rocker look on you, Jill."

"I rather like the way you look right now too."

She smiled seductively then pushed her pubic triangle back up to my mouth. "Isn't it about time for another snack? We wouldn't want you to become undernourished."

I obeyed the goddess Marie's wishes and dined on her exquisite delights. When she began to lose her balance, I scooped her up in my arms and carried her to the bedroom, laying her down on top of the bed covers.

I motioned for her to lie still while I went back to the kitchen and drained the water from the pasta pot. Then I ran back to the bedroom, ripped off the remainder of my clothing, and dove onto the bed. "Dinner's ready, if you're interested."

She smiled at me in what could only be called a "leering" manner. "The spaghetti or the woman?"

"Both, actually."

She pulled me close to her and began kissing and fondling me again. I mounted her body, straddling her hips, and leaned into our kiss. Her fingers found their way inside me where she played me like an instrument. She set all my nerves to vibrating and the crescendo was not long in coming. I collapsed on top of her, but she rolled me over and had her way with me again. Her mouth and hands were amazing. It felt as though she already knew all my trigger spots. She manipulated them with skill and artistry.

When my storehouse of sexual fire was finally spent, I had to stop her from trying to make me excited again.

"Time out!" I croaked, with a throat parched from the loss of fluids.

Marie smirked at me. "Okay, Miss Jill, I'll give you five minutes before I try a few more tricks on you."

I groaned. "God, Marie, I really don't think I can take any more."

"We'll see about that. Why don't I get us some spaghetti while you rest?"

"Sounds like a plan. I'll be there in a minute."

I don't know how long she was gone because I fell asleep before I could muster up the strength to dress and go to the kitchen. It turns out I didn't need to because Marie brought our plates into the bedroom. The next thing I knew, the goddess Marie was standing beside me with a plate of spaghetti in her hands.

"Here you go, dream girl, one plate of nourishing food. We've got a long night ahead of us."

I sat up and smiled at her. She was so beautiful standing there offering me sustenance. So I took of the spaghetti and did eat of it. When I did, my eyes were opened, and I knew that I was naked and that she, the goddess Marie, was naked. But we were not ashamed. We exulted in our nakedness and in the power of the knowledge we had shared with each other through our womanly bodies.

Chapter 8
Roller Coaster Ride

While we ate, I attempted to chat casually with Marie. Chatting, however, was not what Marie had in mind. Instead she teased my breasts with her foot, causing the nipples to harden again in excitement. Then she rolled over ever so casually onto her stomach to eat her dinner. Trying to eat while looking at her naked body was really difficult. So I rolled over too and sat my plate of warm spaghetti on her lovely light brown bottom.

She giggled at this maneuver. "I've never had anyone use my butt for a placemat before."

"I didn't see any other way of finishing my food, if I didn't hide your nakedness from view."

"Don't you like the scenery?"

"Ah, you see, that's the problem. I like the scenery so much that I find it quite distracting. I figure the only way I will manage to consume my dinner is to try to think about doing something other than consuming you."

"But I want you to consume me, Jill," she said in a low, seductive whisper.

"And I want to consume you, but I need a few calories if we're going to be at this for awhile."

"Okay, but you'd better eat fast because I'm almost finished with my spaghetti, and I'm coming after you with a spoon for my dessert."

I groaned and sat up in bed. I set my half-eaten dinner on the dresser and turned my attentions back to the nymphomaniac with whom I was spending the night. "That does it," I announced. "I can't concentrate on my food when this tantalizing dish has been set before my eyes. I want you, Marie. I want to gobble you up completely tonight. I don't even want to leave enough crumbs for a doggy bag."

"Good, because I don't want to be a doggy bag." She rolled over and handed me her empty plate. "No doggy bag needed here either."

I nearly threw her plate at the dresser in my rush to get back to making love to Marie. She had rolled back onto her stomach, so I positioned my body on top of hers and lightly brushed her backside with my breasts. She moaned in enjoyment and allowed me to coat her body with kisses.

After several minutes, she said, "I had forgotten what it was like to enjoy such languorous foreplay."

I paused in my kisses long enough to say, "After what we've already done this evening, I don't think this qualifies as 'foreplay,' technically speaking."

Marie giggled again. "No, I suppose not. Love play then. Lesbians are so generous in their love play."

"Does Enrico not engage in foreplay?"

"Not usually. He's always so hot and ready. I usually just have to get ready fast, so he can plunge in right away before he ejaculates."

"Gosh, it sounds like he hardly needed you at all." I grimaced. "Um, sorry, that didn't come out right. I didn't mean for that to sound so harsh."

"It's okay, Jillie. I have to agree with you. Only, of course, he says I'm the reason he gets hot so fast. But I have to wonder. I don't think he really does need me for that. I think he kind of stays turned on."

"You know, Marie, I don't really think I want to talk about you and Enrico having sex. That's a little hard for me to think about."

"Why?"

"Um, I don't know exactly. It just is. I have been attracted to you pretty much since the moment we first met. When Mr. Watanabe introduced me to you on your first day at work, I suddenly felt weak in the knees."

Marie rolled over beneath me and looked up at me with a knowing smile. "I wondered about that. I felt a psychic shift when you looked at me. It had quite an effect on me, and I could definitely tell that you were affected too. I didn't think anything would ever come of it though. At least not until I had that first dream."

"The one where you had something in your eye?"

"No, actually, Jill, I had a few others before that one." She grinned when my mouth dropped open. She reached up and gently closed it.

"You mean you had other dreams?"

She nodded at me, still grinning slyly.

I climbed to the head of the bed and leaned back against the pillows. "I had other dreams before too, but I can't remember them very well now." Then I looked back at her incredulously. "My god, Marie, why didn't you tell me?"

She rolled her eyes at me. "Oh, be serious, Jill. What was I supposed to say to you? I suspected that you might be attracted to me, but I didn't know for sure. That's not exactly something you bring up over a burrito lunch. I would have been so embarrassed if you hadn't shared the attraction. Besides, I wasn't planning to act on my attraction to you."

"May I ask what changed your mind?"

"I guess it was because I found out that you were having the dreams too. Up until then it was easy to pretend that it was my own private fantasy. When I discovered that you were sharing the dreams, I knew they were the prophetic kind. I fought it at first, but then I thought to myself, 'What the hell? If it happens, it happens.' You know, Jill, I thought you were so sexy the moment I looked into those lesbian eyes of yours. I had hoped I would be able to keep my attraction to you under control, but it seems I couldn't. Now Enrico knows about it too. There's no going back to him. He will never believe me again."

"Believe what?"

"He knew about my lesbian past. As I told you, that's how we met. We were commiserating over the loss of our girlfriends. Before we got married, he asked me if I was still attracted to women. I told him that I was through with women because at that moment I was still really crushed by Theresa's treatment of me. At that time, I sincerely thought that I would never get involved with another woman. "

"What changed your mind?"

"Oh, Jillie, you are too much sometimes. You changed my mind. Haven't you been listening to me?"

"Yeah, so I guess that means that meeting me changed your mind?"

In answer to my question, she sat up and looked at me. I felt a shiver run through me. She leaned over and kissed me very sensuously. I felt my heart melting like wax in the heat of a candle's flame. Marie straddled my lap, allowing me to find entrance into her body again. When she came, she arched her back for several moments, her body shaking with the power of her orgasm. Then she gracefully floated down, her back nestled between my outstretched legs. Her erect nipples gradually melted into the soft mounds of her breasts. Her eyes fluttered then opened. There were tears in them.

"What is it, Marie? Did I hurt you?"

She smiled a sad smile and shook her head.

"What then?"

"I can't do this."

"Can't do what?"

She sat up and hid her face in her hands. She shook her head. "I know I seduced you, but now I feel awful."

"Gee, thanks."

"It's not you, Jill."

"Then what is it, Marie?"

"It's me. It's Enrico and my mother."

"Your mother?"

"Jill, try to understand. My mother is very conservative. She's a devout Catholic, who was so ashamed when I came out as bisexual. She didn't speak to me for weeks. She never let me bring my female lovers home for any length of time. Then she met Enrico, and everything was wonderful again. I went from being the black sheep of the family to being an angel in my mother's eyes. For me to go back to being lesbian, or even bisexual, would simply destroy her."

"So you're going to let your mother emotionally blackmail you into behaving like a heterosexual? Don't you realize that it will never be that way? You were attracted to me after what, a year of marriage to Enrico? Can't you see that if you run away from this attraction, there'll be another and another? You can't run away from who you are."

"I know, Jill, but I'm really confused right now."

I nodded. "That makes two of us."

Just then the phone rang. I debated about letting the answering machine get it, but I decided I needed a breather anyway from this ridiculous scene. I grabbed a flannel shirt from my closet and threw it around my naked torso before heading to the living room to answer the phone. I took a deep breath then picked up the receiver. "Hello?"

A man's voice said, "Is this Jill?"

Just before my mouth could wrap itself around an affirmative answer, my ears recognized the voice as Enrico's. I froze then quietly answered in a higher pitch voice, "Sorry, you have the wrong number." As I replaced the receiver, I heard the voice on the other end yell, "Lying bitch!"

I sat down on the couch and thought about what I should do. I decided to erase the message from my answering machine so my voice wouldn't give me away if he called again. I tried to come up with a false voice to use for the message, and was in the middle of trying to sound more like a man, when Marie came out of the bedroom, wrapped sanctimoniously in my robe.

I looked up, rather startled at her entrance. "Is that robe supposed to act as a chastity belt?" When she looked hurt, I said, "Sorry, I don't mean to lash out at you. You just look so well protected. You don't have to fortify yourself against me, Marie. I'm not a marauding army bent on ravaging you. I will be a perfect gentle-dyke, so don't worry about that." I ran both of my hands through my hair, tugging slightly as I went, inwardly wishing I could scream.

"What's the matter, Jill? You look pale. Why were you talking to yourself?"

"I was trying to come up with a voice that sounded different from my own to leave on my answering machine."

"Why?"

"Because Enrico just called."

"What? How did he get your phone number?"

"Well, if you didn't give it to him, I suspect he just dialed *69. It isn't too difficult these days."

"Oh my God, Jill, I forgot about that. Damn that phone company!"

"Yes, well, they obviously weren't thinking about situations like this when they came up with that handy little feature. I'm surprised it took him this long to think of it."

"God, Jill, I'm so sorry for getting you involved in this. I wouldn't have even used your telephone if I hadn't forgotten my cell phone at home. Maybe I should go to a hotel."

"He has my phone number, Marie, not my address. I can have my number changed. In fact, I'll do that right now." I picked up the phone book, hunted down the service number for Qwest, and then called them to explain my situation. They agreed to change my phone number as quickly as they could, although it might take until tomorrow until it went into effect. Having done that, I started making a list of people I needed to call in the morning with the new number they had given me. I gave Linda's answering machine a quick call in case she tried to call and got worried.

After I hung up the phone, Marie said, "You see, I am causing you problems. I should have left you out of this completely."

"Too late, Marie. I'm already in pretty deep. Even if you leave now, Enrico knows about me. I'd rather have you where I can keep an eye on you. Besides, Linda is going to have a friend, a retired cop, watching my house for a while. It will be easier for him if we stay together, since there's only one of him and two of us."

I ran my hands through my hair again and let out a long sigh. Then I walked back to the bedroom to find something more substantial to wear. Jolly, perhaps sensing my depression, followed me to the bedroom and offered me her head to pet. I sat down on the bed and patted for her to jump up beside me. I leaned over and hugged her furry body. "You're such a faithful friend. I know I can count on you not to mess with my head."

When I sat up again, I realized that Marie was standing in the doorway. "God, Jillie, I'm so sorry. I'm not trying to mess with your head. It's just that my head is already so messed up. I guess I can't help but spread it to others. I suppose I'm playing with Enrico's head too. He doesn't deserve this. He tried to get me to think about my attraction to women before we got married. I thought he was just being insecure at the time. I guess he was being wiser than I was. Maybe he had me figured out better than I did. I really hate hurting him. Now I'm hurting both of you."

I walked over to the closet in search of more modest attire. "No, Marie, I should've known better than to get involved with you before you had time to think all this through. I should have listened to my intuition and not kissed you."

Marie continued to stand in the doorway, watching my every move, her eyes roaming over my body.

"Marie?"

Her eyes slowly rose to meet mine. "Yes, Jillie?"

"Please don't look at me like that. I have no self-control when it comes to you. I feel like one of Pavlov's dogs. As soon as you look at me like that, I start to salivate from more than one orifice. Have mercy on me and leave the room so I can find my own chastity belt."

She walked further into the room. Then she sat down on the bed. She stroked Jolly's head for a minute then bent down and whispered something in her ear. Fickle friend that she is, she jumped down and trotted back out to the living room.

"What did you say to her?"

Marie shook her head at me and lay back on the bed. Then before my unbelieving eyes, she laid open the bathrobe and allowed me to look once again upon the radiant beauty of the goddess Marie. I groaned and felt my knees weaken. After another hour of lovemaking, we finally came up for air.

Afterwards, I opted to take a shower to freshen up. As I headed in that direction, the telephone rang again. I picked it up and answered in as manly a voice as I could muster and was relieved to learn that it was Linda returning my call. I handed the phone to Marie, who was retying my bathrobe around her body, so she could tell her about the telephone incident with Enrico. Then I went ahead and took a shower. When I came out of the bathroom, Marie relayed that Linda had already dispatched Mack to watch the house. I peeked through the blinds on the front window and noticed a dark green Jetta that I'd never seen before in the neighborhood. There was a large man sitting in the front seat, though I couldn't positively identify him as Mack.

I turned to Marie. "I think our bodyguard has arrived. That is, unless Enrico drives a Volkswagen Jetta."

"No, he has a black Chevy Nova."

"What year?"

"I have no idea. Old, though."

"An old black Chevy Nova. Got'cha."

"I feel like I'm in a movie or something."

I nodded. "Or a mystery novel. We've got a retired cop turned detective out there keeping an eye on us. We have a jealous husband who is battering his wife."

"Jill, please," Marie smiled politely at me. "Could you stop with the melodrama? This is difficult enough already. Don't forget that this is my life we're talking about here." She sighed and plunked down on the recliner by the front window. She peeked carefully through the blinds. "God, I'm tired of this already. I feel tense just thinking about Enrico."

I walked over to her and, leaning over the back of the recliner, massaged her shoulders for a few minutes. "You need to get some sleep." She arched her neck to look up at me. I leaned over farther and kissed her lightly on the forehead. "I think I'm going to head that way myself." I started walking towards the bedroom, but stopped in the hallway before continuing.

"Help yourself to the shower, if you need it. There are towels in the linen closet. Lots of shampoo and toothpaste in the bathroom. I'm suddenly very exhausted. Goodnight. Wake me up if you need anything. Jolly usually sleeps at the foot of the bed, but you can push her off if you don't have enough room. Oh, and just for the record, I was originally planning to sleep in the guestroom, so you could have the bed to yourself, in an effort to be gallant and all. But I'm assuming that is no longer necessary. I'm sorry to crash like this suddenly, but I didn't get a lot of sleep last night and this evening's activities have sort of exhausted me. "

Marie smiled a fragile smile at me. "I can just sleep here on the couch."

My mind suddenly woke up again. "What? Why would you do that?"

"I don't want to impose on you."

I started laughing so hard that I slid down the wall in the hallway and just sat there for a few minutes. Jolly came and lapped at my face, not certain if I were laughing or crying. I wasn't completely certain myself.

"Why are you laughing?"

Finally I was able to say, "I don't know. That just seemed funny to me. I hope I didn't hurt your feelings. We seem to keep missing each other emotionally, in spite of the connection we have created between us sexually. Have I been anything but utterly candid about how I feel about you?"

When Marie didn't answer, I said, "For god's sake, woman, I love you. I adore you. I would do anything for you. How could you possibly impose on me by allowing your body to sleep next to mine tonight or any other night?"

Marie looked at me with a puzzled expression.

I stood up and reached out my hands to her. "Look, Marie, I realize that you may not share my love, even if you do share the sexual attraction. I know that sex doesn't equal love. I could have lived my entire life loving you from afar. Now that you have come into my house, if only for a night, and allowed me to express my heartfelt attraction to you, how could I feel put out? I'm trying not to roll myself out onto the floor before your feet, just so I can cushion your footfalls. Trust me; you're not imposing on me. You've shared my food, my dog, and my body. Come and share my dreams again, this time under the same roof. I want to be the one to be awakened by the heat of your passionate dreams."

She nodded solemnly then headed for the bathroom.

As I crawled under the covers, Jolly jumped up beside me. I looked to her for some sage canine advice. "Women! Who does understand them, I wonder?" She licked my face then headed for the foot of the bed. She pawed at the covers, turned around a couple times to make sure she was positioned exactly right, and then plopped down. As I drifted off to sleep, I heard Jolly unleash a contented sigh.

I immediately fell into an exhausted, dreamless slumber. When I awoke, I checked the clock to see how long I had until my alarm went off. It was 3:30 a.m., so I rolled over to go back to sleep. Then I suddenly realized that Marie wasn't in the bed with me. I got up and stumbled sleepily towards the bathroom. On my way back through, I realized that Marie had indeed gone to sleep on the couch. Jolly was curled up on the floor next to her with her head carefully positioned under the hand Marie had draped over the edge.

Hmm. I guess Marie's got a human bodyguard outside and a canine one inside.

I dug a fleece blanket out of the closet and went to cover Marie's small, sleeping figure. Jolly got up and went to get a drink of water while I tended to Marie. I guess she figured that her charge would be safe in my care while she took a little break. When I tucked Marie in, she murmured something incomprehensible and rolled over to face the back of the couch. I bent over and lightly kissed her delicately carved ear. *What a gem you are, Marie, a precious gem.*

I was about to head back to bed when I heard a car door slam somewhere in the neighborhood. I peeked through the blinds to see if I could see anything but there was nothing interesting to see. It was only a neighbor coming in from a late night at work. I knew the guy well enough to know that he worked the night shift somewhere, but not well enough to know where. We'd met at a neighborhood watch meeting a couple years ago, but I had long since forgotten his name.

Wide awake now, I picked up a copy of *Outside* magazine from the coffee table and started leafing through it. I was pretty sure I'd already read the whole thing, but figured I'd look at the pictures until I got sleepy again, which I assumed would be pretty soon. When I headed for bed again, I heard Marie stir on the couch. I turned to look at her while she sat up and stretched. I approached her and tenderly kissed her mussed hair.

"What time is it? Is it time to get ready for work?" She asked in a sleepy voice.

"No, there's plenty of night left before dawn. What time do you usually get up?"

"I don't have to get up until seven. I always go back to sleep after Enrico leaves at six."

"Then go back to sleep."

She nodded, so I turned back to head for my own bed while Jolly returned to her post by Marie's side.

"Jillie?"

I stopped and waited for her to continue. "Yes?"

"Would you hold me?"

I turned back towards my sleepy-faced lover and smiled at her. "Of course. Would you like for me to hold you on the couch or would the bed be more comfortable?"

She got up and headed towards me, so I reached out my hand and took hers. Then I escorted her to my bedroom with Jolly following closely behind us. I turned down the covers for Marie then went around and crawled into bed next to her. Her flesh felt cool against my skin. I wrapped my body around hers like a blanket then fell asleep listening to the gentle rhythm of her breathing.

When morning dawned, I awakened with the feeling you get after a night of satisfying sex. There was a smile on my face that I couldn't wipe off, in spite of the fact that I knew that my life wasn't exactly in the best shape at the moment. I knew that Marie was feeling conflicted about her sexuality and her marriage. I knew that I thought she should choose me over living with a violent man who had already given her one black eye. I also knew that wasn't likely. In reality, I suspected that Marie would return to Enrico, beg his forgiveness, and go on as before.

Perhaps she would remember our night together fondly. Keep it as a safeguard against the cold brutality of a world insensitive to the drama being staged within the confines of Marie's soul. Perhaps she would call me one day, after many months and a few glasses of wine, and try to talk to me as though we were just old friends. I knew that I would never be able to treat her as I had before, as though I had not been granted access to the sacred well of her sensuality. How does one pretend to live a normal life after partaking of the lips of a goddess? Mere mortality wasn't all it was cracked up to be once you've tasted of the divine.

It was obvious to me that I was feeling this way because it had been way too long since I had last bedded such a willing and uninhibited sexual partner. But there was something else, and Goddess help my soul, that something was love, and I knew it all too well.

Would that I could cut myself and shed the sacrificial blood that would make it possible for me to walk away from the sin of my desire for this sublime sexual love. Would that I could even regret my actions of loving a woman with a wedding band around her finger. But I had been a lesbian far too long not to realize that this talisman can be nothing more than a tightening noose around a finger that leads to a heart that is alive and pumping healthy blood. Left in place too long, a ring that doesn't fit its wearer can cut off that life sustaining flow from the heart. Once removed, the imprint left behind would eventually fade away with time.

Yet how long would this woman have to wait? More to the point, would this noose ever be removed from the hand of the woman who had stolen my heart? Only time would tell, and at this moment, the grains of sand were annoyingly mute. So I continued smiling as I went about my morning rituals, silently basking in the opportunity to adapt myself to the presence of Marie in my house, in my morning, and in my waking world.

Chapter 9

Morning Aftermath

After an omelet and some toast with jam, Marie and I decided to drive to work together in my car, leaving her car hidden under the tarp. I turned on the radio hoping to provide some distraction from the weirdness of our present situation. Marie lapsed into a thoughtful silence, while I managed to drive unconsciously to work, allowing my mind to replay some of last night's more salient moments.

Startled to have arrived at our place of employment so quickly, I glanced over at my silent partner and smiled. "Say, are you in there somewhere?"

Marie smiled sadly at me. "I'm here, but I don't feel very good."

"What's the matter?"

"Stress, I think. I feel all knotted up inside. What if Enrico comes to work today?"

"Hmm. I guess I hadn't really thought about that. Maybe I should talk to Mr. Watanabe. He seemed to be genuinely concerned about you yesterday. Perhaps he can keep an eye out for Enrico and circumvent any touchy situations."

"That's a good idea, but I suppose I should be the one to talk to him. He might think it's funny that you're so involved in my personal life."

"Okay, but I don't think you have to worry about him. He's a very kind and compassionate man."

"I would still feel better if I told him what is going on here. It's my responsibility."

I held my hands up in surrender. "No problem. I'll leave it up to you."

"Thanks for being so sweet about all this. I've really put you in a bad position. I'm sorry about that."

I reached over and placed my hand over Marie's. "It's my pleasure, really."

Marie blushed at the intimacy of my actions, gathered up her belongings, and made a swift exit from the car. I got out and followed two steps behind her, thinking that Marie might not want it to look as though we'd come in together.

I reached out quickly as we arrived at the door and swung it open for her. Marie smiled at me again and stepped into the hallway before me. I headed for my office while Marie dumped her jacket and purse on her desk then headed in the direction of Mr. Watanabe's office.

As lunchtime rolled around, I decided that I'd better offer to take Marie out to lunch, since she didn't have her own transportation. I ran into Mr. Watanabe on my way to Marie's desk. He made a slight bowing motion and gestured for me to accompany him. As we walked towards his office, he spoke in a low voice. "Marie has told me some things about her husband."

I nodded, not sure how much she'd told him.

"She should be safe here, since her desk is surrounded by several others. I have informed our sales staff about the possibility of a security problem. Everyone has agreed to watch for signs of trouble."

I nodded again when he paused for a moment. He walked into his office and held out a chair for me. I sat down, but Mr. Watanabe remained standing. He looked very concerned as he continued. "My daughter had to have a restraining order issued against her husband. Has Marie seen a lawyer yet?"

"No, but she has an appointment after work today. Yesterday she talked to a social worker who referred her to a lawyer she uses for her clients who are in imminent danger."

"Good, good. If this Enrico is as dangerous as he sounds, she will need to do all the legal paperwork as quickly as possible. Without it, I cannot summon the police until he does something wrong. It may be too late, if I have to wait until that moment. With a restraining order, any of us can call the police the moment he steps onto this property. Please encourage her to take care of this today."

I smiled at him and nodded again. "I'll do what I can, though I don't know how much influence I have over Marie."

Mr. Watanabe looked me in the eyes directly. "Your influence in regards to Ms. Garcia is considerable. She will listen to you, I think." He smiled and bowed in a way that let me know that it was time for me to take my leave. As I exited, he said, "Please let me know if there is any way I may assist you or Ms. Garcia. I am fond of you girls. I'd hate to see you come to harm."

I smiled warmly. "Thank you, Mr. Watanabe. I really appreciate your concern. I'm sure Marie does too."

He merely smiled and nodded.

As I headed out of his office, his words whirled around in my head. I couldn't figure out if Marie had told him something, he had figured out about us, or if I was just a great big paranoid lesbian. Whatever the case, we had support from a very important man. I was certain that no harm would come to Marie while she was at work.

When I got to Marie's office, I was chagrined to find her absent. Turning towards Candace, I asked, "You wouldn't happen to know where Marie is, would you?" I smiled my friendliest smile in her direction.

"Bathroom, I think," she said, nodding back towards the ladies room across the cubicle area.

"Oh, good. I'll just get some water and wait for her return then."

"Mmm," was the only response I got, as Candace went back to concentrating on the papers in front of her.

Moments later, Marie emerged from the restroom. She was holding her stomach with one hand and steadying herself against the wall with the other one. "Hi, Jill," she said weakly, "What are you doing here?"

"I thought I'd see if I could take you to lunch."

Marie smiled weakly at me. "No, I think I'll eat here."

"What on earth are you going to eat? You didn't pack a lunch today."

Marie glanced around the room, as though she were checking to see if anyone was paying attention to our conversation. I felt a slight chill in the air.

"I usually keep a little something in my desk drawers. Anyway, I'm not hungry today. But don't let me stop you from going out. I'll be fine. Thanks for your concern."

Her professionally polite tone sent another chill down my spine. "Okay, well, maybe I'll see you later then."

"Yes, perhaps."

As I walked out to my car, I thought hard about Marie's behavior. It was quite apparent that she didn't want to let anyone know that she and I were anything except friendly co-workers. Her ability to run hot and cold was rather disturbing. While I agreed with a discreet approach to our relationship while at work, I wasn't exactly secure in the knowledge that it wouldn't be painfully polite outside work as well. I may have been nourishing warm, loving thoughts about her all day, but she'd obviously spent the morning building barriers to keep me at a distance.

After a quick bite at the deli, I headed back to the office, determined to give Linda a call as soon as I got a free moment. When I finally got through to her, she seemed glad to hear from me. She told me that Mack had reported no suspicious activity near my house last night. I was relieved to hear this, though not necessarily surprised, since I knew Enrico hadn't a clue where I lived. It wasn't as though he could just drive up and down every street in King County looking for Marie's car.

Linda promised to keep her cell phone nearby until she heard from us after Marie's visit to the lawyer. She also assured me that Mack would be on duty again tonight. When I mentioned that Marie may not want to stay with me again, Linda saw through my ruse.

"What happened last night to change her mind? Or is that none of my business?"

"I-uh, well, I'm not sure exactly, but she seems really distant today."

"She has a lot on her mind. Was she different, I mean, less distant last night?"

"Well, you could say that we got quite close last night."

"I see."

"Yep, I suppose you do. I can't elaborate now, but let's just say that her faucet runs either very cold or very hot."

I couldn't stop myself from smiling when I heard Linda chuckling on the other end of the line.

"Hmm. Well, okay, that does make things a little more interesting. I'd really prefer if she stayed with you so Mack can keep an eye on both of you, but perhaps I can call in another favor or two and arrange for protection at two different locations. Any idea where else she might stay?"

"No, her folks live in Yakima. She can hardly commute to work from there. I don't get the feeling that she has lots of friends in this area. She and Enrico haven't lived in the Seattle area for very long. They moved here from California, although I think Marie's family is originally from eastern Washington. At least they've been there for a long time. Her father's a dentist."

"A dentist, huh? So I bet she has really clean breath, what with being able to get free cleanings and all."

"Linda, I can't believe we're discussing Marie's breath. Am I imagining things, or are you being just a teensy bit voyeuristic?"

Linda burst into laughter at this. "I suppose I am. Imagine that. Ahem. I guess my own life has grown too dull for words, at least in the love department."

"Yeah, whatever happened to what's-his-name? Jack, wasn't it?"

"Love, it was Mack, and he was at your house last night, as I seem to recall."

"Oh, well, sorry about that. I sure don't mean to take him away from you."

Linda laughed lightly into my ear. "You're not, Jill, darling. We went our separate ways months ago, sort of."

"Sort of? What exactly does that mean?"

"Well, we see each other on a casual, friendly basis on occasion, but the romantic part never did work out as well as we could've hoped. Nothing tragic, just not enough spark to keep the fire blazing. A flash-in-the-pan kind of romance really. Very spectacular for its brief moment in time, and then it was over. End of story."

"Well, too bad. He looks like a handsome enough guy from the picture you showed me yesterday."

"He's a hunk all right, darling, but not very deep. Or too deep, perhaps, I'm not sure which. We definitely didn't make a good match."

"No one since Mack?"

"I'm afraid not. It's just as well, though. I am enjoying not having shaved whisker remnants in my bathroom sink. I think I must be too tidy a person to be able to live with a man. At least not any straight ones I know."

"Yes, what you need is a nice, neat gay man to make your life complete."

Linda laughed. "Isn't life ironic? I've been tempted to place a classified ad for a neat middle-aged man, but I'm afraid I'd get Felix Unger. That would be just a bit too much. And he really was gay too, wasn't he?"

"Well, not officially, according to the script. But had he been a real life character, I wouldn't have been convinced that he was straight."

"Yes, my thoughts exactly. Who knows, maybe I should find a nice woman and settle down?"

I nearly choked. "Er, yes, well then, be sure to advertise for a neat lesbian."

"Lesbians aren't messy, are they?"

I laughed out loud. "Some of them are."

"But you're not."

"I have my moments, but no, not for the most part." I ran a hand through my hair and shook my head at my old friend. "Well, Linda, I need to go and pretend that I'm getting something accomplished."

"Not doing too well then?"

"I feel fine, but between my memories of last night's activities and the cold awakening of the morning after, I don't know what to think. This whole thing is wreaking havoc on my ability to concentrate."

"Yes, well, try not to be too hard on yourself or Marie. She's got a lot to think about, and really, last night might have been...well, a reaction."

"Quite a reaction at that. More like an overreaction. Thanks for the encouragement."

"Oh, Jill, darling, I don't mean to dash cold water on your passionate feelings, but that woman has an awful lot to think about right now. She doesn't really have room for a beautiful distraction like you."

"You know, Linda, you sure know how to dash a gal's hope with panache. Who could be offended by someone telling them they'd better play it cool because their beauty is distracting someone from the task of breaking up their marriage? When you put it that way, I feel like a perfect cad. Beautiful, of course, but a cad, nonetheless."

"Thank you, Jill, darling. Your sense of humor is so refreshing. Say, why didn't you ever try to seduce me in college. You've always been so charming and such an adorable lesbian."

I was momentarily stunned by this suggestion.

"Jill? Are you still breathing?"

"Er, I think so. I just can't believe you said that. Are you kidding me? I always thought you were utterly heterosexual. I had no idea you'd ever consider such a thing. Is this the first time it's ever crossed your mind?"

"Of course not. I think most women wonder at one time or another what it would be like to be with another woman in that way. And, you know, lesbians are everywhere these days. Not that they haven't been before, but you know what I mean. They're so popular now, what with Ellen DeGeneres, Melissa Etheridge, and the L Word. All those wonderful, beautiful women, so powerful, so vibrant, so alive. It's positively stimulating."

"Yes, well, I'm certainly feeling stimulated now. Perhaps we should leave this discussion for another time. I now have more things to think about than I can possibly keep tucked inside my head for the rest of the afternoon."

"Are you trying to avoid answering my question?"

I cleared my throat in an effort to stall for time. "It's just that I, uh, never entertained that scenario as a possibility in our relationship. Obviously a terrible oversight on my part."

"Obviously. I'll let you off the hook for now, Jill darling. I've got to run. I have an appointment in a few minutes. It was so nice chatting with you. Do give me a ring later on to let me know how things are going."

"It's a promise and, Linda, thanks for all your support. I don't know what I'd do without you."

"That's something of a consolation, at least. Ta ta."

"Bye."

I hung up the phone and ran both hands through my hair. "Aaaaiiiiiiyyyyyy!" I put my head on my desk for a moment in an attempt to gather my thoughts. I jumped at the knock on my door. I looked up to find Marie standing in the doorway, clutching her stomach. Her face was pale. "What's wrong, Marie?"

Marie shook her head and slumped against the wall. "I don't know. I just feel sick."

"Is it the flu or your nerves?"

"I don't know. I feel like I'm going to throw up, but I can't. I'm all jittery."

I frowned at her, while trying to think of what to do. "Maybe we should get you to a doctor after your appointment with the lawyer."

She looked at me and smiled. "Or maybe I won't need a doctor after I see the lawyer. It could just be stress."

"There's no chance you're pregnant, is there?"

Marie looked slightly alarmed. "No, I don't think so, but contraceptives aren't totally foolproof."

I nodded and reached up to tug on my hair.

"Stay calm, Jill. I don't think I need to see a doctor just yet, but I will if this nausea doesn't go away. Maybe we could stop at the drugstore to get a pregnancy test before we go home after my appointment with the lawyer."

"Go home? You mean you want to go home with me again tonight?"

Marie looked embarrassed. "Well, if it wouldn't be too much trouble. I don't want to put you out, but my car is over there. I will need to find a way to go to my house for more clothes at some point, since I don't know how many more of your shirts will fit me. But I don't want to go without some protection."

I scrutinized her attire carefully. "Is that my shirt? I thought it looked familiar, but it's been years since I wore it last. I'm glad it fits you. I totally forgot about your needing a change of clothing. I wish you would have said something."

My face must have registered the puzzlement I was feeling at the moment because Marie said, "What's wrong, Jillie? Have I overstepped my boundaries?"

"Oh no, it's not that. It's just that, well, I don't know what it is, this whole situation, I guess. I don't know what to do now. With you, I mean. We need to get your clothes, but I don't want you anywhere near Enrico. You could be pregnant with his baby. Then what? I mean, what do you do about that? I don't usually have to worry about the woman I love getting pregnant. I'm not at all prepared for this kind of situation. I don't know what to do."

"Jill, it's all right. Slow down. It may just be tension. It may be the flu. I need to get something to eat, something bland. Then we need to go to the lawyer's office. After that, we can get a pregnancy test and find out if I'm really pregnant. Then we decide what to do after that point, if there is a decision to be made."

I found it interesting that she was including me in her decision process about her possible pregnancy. It was puzzling. I could not figure this woman out to save my life. First, she's giving me the cold shoulder about lunch then she's talking about making decisions with me about her pregnancy. Of course, the lunch thing may have just been because she was feeling sick. She definitely hadn't looked well at the time, but I just chalked that up to nerves, not morning sickness.

I made myself pause for a moment and take a deep breath. I tried to calm my thoughts and focus on the tasks at hand. "Okay. So we need to go to the lawyer's office to get the restraining order arranged. Then we should figure out how to get your clothes. But say, I could go get the pregnancy test while you're with the lawyer. That would save time."

"Well, if you really want to, Jill, but you don't have to do that for me."

"No, no, I'll take care of that."

She smiled tenderly at me when I helped her into her jacket, and we headed out the door.

While we were driving to Bellevue, I kept thinking about the possible complications that could arise from the pregnancy, the emotional and legal ones. If she is pregnant, then she will have to tell Enrico, since he's the father. Even if they separated or divorced, she'd probably have to let him have visitation rights. That would mean he would have to stay in contact with her. That would also mean that he'd have the opportunity to kidnap the baby and turn her life into a living hell. It would also give him ample opportunity to kill one or both of us. How does custody work when one parent has a restraining order against the other?

"Jillie?"

I snapped back to the present. "Yes?"

"Are you okay?"

"Yes, I'm okay. My voice sounded shrill. "Why?"

"Well, you're beating your thumb against the steering wheel rather hard and fast, so either you've got a wild tune in your head, or you're really uptight about something."

I willed my fingers to stop banging against the steering wheel. "Um, yeah, I was thinking about that old surfing song, 'Wipe-out.'"

Marie smiled at me and shook her head. "You are a terrible liar, Jillie."

I blushed. "Yeah, so I am. Linda used to tell me that all the time. I could never skip classes in college because I couldn't lie."

"Good. I don't want to be with any more liars."

"What is that supposed to mean?"

"It means, Jill, that I don't want to be with someone who is a good liar. I don't want to be lied to any more."

"So Enrico lied to you?"

"Both Enrico and Theresa. I can't believe I went from one bull-shitter to another. I can't stand being lied to. It's like the ultimate insult. It means that a person doesn't trust you with the truth."

"Oh, sorry. I was trying not to make you feel bad. But, yes, I'm a little uptight. I, uh, don't know what to do or say to you. I don't know where I stand. I love you so much, and I don't know how you feel about me. I don't know if you're going to decide that you don't want to be a lesbian any more. I don't want to cause you to be ashamed of yourself or what we do in bed together. But I also know that I can't change how you feel. I'm totally powerless in this whole situation.

"I think about your naked body and how you feel in my arms. Then I think about Enrico or your mother. I remember how you broke down after we made love, and how you said that you just couldn't go back to being lesbian because you wanted your mother's approval. I can't change your mother's mind about us, Marie, but I also can't help but love you. I'm so completely miserable and happy all at the same time, and I don't know what to do about it. I don't think there is anything I can do about it.

"I'm so afraid that if you're pregnant, then Enrico wins somehow. You will either go back to him, or you will have to spend the next twenty years sharing custody of the child you created together. That scares me, and it makes me angry, because I don't want him to have any leverage over you."

I didn't realize that I had started crying until my vision became so blurred that it was difficult for me to see to drive. I managed to catch my turnoff, however, and pulled into the parking lot of the lawyer's office and turned off the car. My whole body shook with the anguished sobs that were escaping from my tensed body. Marie's hand was resting on my arm, and I realized at some point that she was crying as hard as I was.

As my tears subsided, and I was able to regain my composure somewhat, I reached for the tissues in the backseat of my car. "I'm so sorry, Marie. I shouldn't have touched you last night. You're not ready for that yet. You may not ever be ready for that again. I just couldn't resist you."

Marie smiled at me and wiped her tears away with her hands. "I'm the one who should be sorry, Jill, but I'm not. I really enjoyed last night, and I know I've been acting like a crazy woman, but it's just been so difficult. It's like I've been trying so hard to pretend to be straight so my mother would love me and accept me. But I've also realized that if she's going to love me and accept me, then she's going to have to love who I am, not just who she wants me to be.

"Our lovemaking last night proved to me that I am lesbian. Since I've been with you, I've seen that there is a woman in this world who can and will love me the way I want to be loved. Who will please me as I wish to be pleased, and who will take my hand and help me to face the world and all its complications and prejudices.

"Even if my mother decides to reject me completely, I can't turn my back on what I feel for you, Jill. I do love you. I'm sorry my life is so complicated right now, but it won't always be this way. I know it's wrong to ask you to hang on until I can get it straightened out, but I want you to stay by me. I want you to help me get through this.

"If I am pregnant, then I will keep that fact secret from Enrico. He doesn't have to know. I'll swear in a court of law that I had another lover, if I have to, in order to keep him away from our life together. If I am to raise a child, then I don't want that child to be associated with a man such as Enrico. After what he did to me the other night, he doesn't even deserve to know that he's a father. I wouldn't want my child to know him."

I leaned over to hug Marie, and she leaned into my arms. "Oh, Marie, I will stay with you, no matter what happens. We'll get through all of this somehow."

When she pulled away from my embrace, I figured she was getting ready to go into the lawyer's office. Instead she looked in my eyes. "Please don't leave me to go to the drugstore. That can wait. I'd like for you to go in to see the lawyer with me. This is as much your business now as it is mine. I need your support, and I'd like for you to hear firsthand what she has to say."

I nodded, tears pouring down my cheeks again. Marie reached up and wiped them away. Then she leaned towards me and planted a soft kiss on my lips. I kissed her back tenderly. "I love you, Marie. I'd be glad to go with you."

"Jillie?"

"Yes?"

"Thank you for being so open and honest with me. I knew you were upset, but I need for you to trust me with your thoughts and feelings. Don't shut me out. I may not look very strong, but I can be pretty tough when I need to be."

I smiled back at her and squeezed her hand. Then we headed inside to talk to the lawyer.

Chapter 10
Taking Charge

The visit with the lawyer was anti-climatic after the emotional scene in the car. Although she lacked Linda's exuberance, the lawyer was very kind and helpful. She listened intently while Marie told her story. She offered Marie tissues when she began to cry, while she was telling the story of Enrico's forced sexual advances. She listened carefully to everything Marie said and didn't say.

When she had heard enough of Marie's story, she began to ask probing questions about our relationship. She had accurately guessed the nature of our feelings for one another. She cautioned us about not flaunting our relationship in front of Enrico. She recommended issuing a restraining order against him as soon as possible. She felt that we were both in danger of bodily harm. She was relieved to hear that Linda's friend, Mack, was keeping an eye on us for the time being. When all the legal details had been ironed out, and Marie had signed all the papers and answered all the questions, we finally took our leave.

We walked solemnly out to the car. Wordlessly we got into my car, and I pulled out into the traffic. We eased our way onto the freeway and slipped over into the car pool lane. Traffic was duly congested for the time of day, but we managed to get through it pretty quickly in the transit lane. I pulled into the parking lot of Bartell's Drugstore. Marie and I went in together. After we had walked up and down a couple aisles, a clerk approached and asked if she could help.

Marie smiled politely. "I need a pregnancy test."

The clerk nodded and took off to the other side of the store. She waved us over. "Here you go. Is this your first?" She smiled kindly at both of us.

I looked blankly at her, unable to fathom why she was asking us such a question, wondering what was in her mind.

Marie spoke up and much to my surprise said, "Yes, but we're hoping to have a couple more eventually." She slipped her arm under mine.

The clerk smiled widely and said, "Oh, how wonderful for you. I hope you get good news!"

I stared down at the top of Marie's head, completely stunned. After she'd paid the friendly clerk, we headed back towards the car. "What was that all about?"

"Oh, Jill, she was just being friendly, and I wasn't about to tell her the real situation. It just wasn't worth the emotional effort, and it wasn't any of her business. She was only being polite anyway. I'm certain she wouldn't have wanted to know the truth. Let her think we're a happy middle-class lesbian couple off to populate the earth."

I shook my head at her. "You always surprise me."

"You see, I told you I could be tough. I was protecting myself, and all she wanted was to hear a pleasant story about how nice the world is now that lesbians are having babies together."

"Whoa! That was caustic."

"I'm sorry. It's been a hard day for both of us. Do you think less of me because I dodged that awkward situation?"

"Do you feel awkward about us?"

"No, why do you ask?"

"Well, I know you weren't feeling well this afternoon, but you were really cool when I went to check on you, and Candace had told me you were in the bathroom."

"Jillie, I don't talk to Candace about anything personal. I've never even mentioned Enrico to her. She's the last person I would confide in about anything. I don't really trust her. I guess it's because I've heard her gossiping about some of the other girls at the office. I can't stand that. Around her, I'll probably treat you like a mere acquaintance, but it's because of her not you and me. I'm sorry if I hurt your feelings. I didn't mean to."

"No, I, well, a little bit, but I chalked it up to your sick stomach. Are you feeling any better now that we talked to the lawyer? Or is your stomach still upset?"

"My stomach is still a little iffy, but at the moment, I'm with you, and that feels really good. I'm not too thrilled about the interview with the lawyer, and I'm definitely not happy with my life the way it is right now. I don't even know what to do about my clothes. I don't have anything else to wear tomorrow. I've already worn these slacks two days in a row. I feel really uncomfortable about all that."

"Do you want to go get Mack and head over there?"

"I don't know. I guess so. I don't know what else to do. I didn't happen to notice any dresses or skirts in your closet when I was looking for a top to wear. You're a lot taller than me, so it's not like I could borrow any of your slacks. "

This mental picture put a smile on my face. "No, I suppose not. So let's go ask Mack what he thinks we should do. But first, would you like to get a bite to eat? I'm not really in the mood to dine out, but I'm also not in the mood to cook dinner, and I still haven't gone to the grocery store. I feel emotionally drained. I can't imagine you feel any better."

"How about take-out?"

"What did you have in mind? There's a great Mexican restaurant near my house."

"Sure. I haven't had any good Mexican food lately, but we have to get it to go. I'm a little afraid to be out in public a lot right now."

"Right, you don't want Enrico to see you. No problem."

We pulled into the parking lot of Torero's and sat there for a couple seconds. Neither of us seemed anxious to jump out and order dinner. I glanced over at Marie. Her brows were furrowed as though she were lost in intense thought. "Earth to Marie. Come in, please."

She smiled at me sadly. "Sorry. I was just thinking about what I would do if I found out that I was pregnant. I mean, it's not the baby's fault that the father is a jerk."

I patted her arm. "No, it's not the baby's fault. Any baby of yours would be beautiful and wonderful. It doesn't matter so much about the father. It would be you raising it."

"So you think I should keep it?" She raised her eyebrows in wonder.

"I think you should do whatever you want to do about it. But first, I think you should find out if you're pregnant. It might be a moot point."

She smiled a brighter smile. "Yes, I suppose so."

"Okay, that's settled. Now are you ready to go order some dinner or have your cravings changed to something more along the lines of pickles and ice cream?"

Marie giggled. "Oh, Jillie, you are so funny. I am so glad I have someone like you looking out for me. You make me laugh in spite of all this craziness."

"Good. I'm glad I can make you laugh, Marie. The world sucks if you can't have a good laugh at yourself every once in a while. So are you ready for Mexican or not?"

"Um, I think I changed my mind. Isn't there a Thai restaurant somewhere around here?"

"Just up the road. Is that what you want then?"

"If that's all right with you."

"Yeah, I love Thai cuisine. Let's go." I put the car in reverse and wheeled around to head for our new destination. When we got near the restaurant, I pointed at it. "Have you been here before?"

She shook her head.

"It's really good. I haven't eaten here lately, but I used to go here all the time. What's your favorite Thai dish?"

Marie smiled shyly. "I haven't eaten at very many Thai restaurants, so I really couldn't say. I just felt like having something totally different. Enrico hates Thai food, so I figured it would be a safe place to go. Torero's is one of his favorite places to eat."

"Oh. I hadn't thought of that."

Marie nodded solemnly.

"Ah well. We'll just cross that off our list of possible places to eat for now. Do you want to get our food to go?"

"No, let's go inside. Enrico isn't going to show up here for dinner."

I pulled into the parking lot and looked all around the area before I hit the button to unlock the doors. "Looks like the coast is clear."

Marie looked at me with a puzzled expression. "What does that mean, anyway? I've heard that expression before, but it doesn't make sense to me."

"I don't know. Probably an expression from some war or another. I've never really thought about it before."

We were seated at a table and duly served with menus. I went for my old standby, Phud Thai. Marie chose a chicken cashew dish.

While we ate, I thought about Marie's predicament. I must've been scowling in my concentration, because Marie nudged me slightly with her foot. My train of thought broken, I looked under the table to see what was going on.

Marie laughed. "Now I understand that expression 'deep in thought.' Where were you just now?"

I shook my head and smiled at her. "Just trying to figure out what we're going to do to resolve this situation."

Marie nodded but remained silent.

"I'm sorry. I didn't mean to abandon you in my mental musings."

Marie smiled slightly. "It's okay, Jillie. I still feel guilty about involving you in this mess."

"I think I did a good job of involving myself. You can't blame yourself for that. I wanted those dreams, and I wanted even more for them to become a reality. I just had no idea they would take on such a nightmare quality."

"Yes, I know. This does feel rather nightmarish at times. I'm so sorry."

"Stop! You're making me nuts with all the apologizing. You aren't responsible for all this. Enrico certainly has a share in the nightmare portion of our waking reality."

Marie smiled slightly. "I guess I feel a little foolish for thinking that I could give up my attraction to women. It's like I wrote off all women just because the one I'd chosen last turned out to be a cheating, lying bitch."

"You mean to say that Theresa was cheating on you?"

"Yes, more than once."

I shook my head in disbelief. "I really don't get that. Why would anyone cheat on you?"

Marie shrugged. "I don't know. Why does anyone cheat on anyone? Technically I'm cheating right now on Enrico."

"Ah, true, but you left him before you cheated on him."

Marie sighed and put her fork down. "Not in my heart, Jill. I cheated on him in my dreams and definitely in my thoughts. Because Enrico was always hot and ready for sex, I often found the need to fantasize that I was with a woman in order to catch up with his aroused state. That was the only way I could open up on the inside quickly enough for me to enjoy our sexual encounters, which were frequent. Sometimes I wondered if Enrico was addicted to sex. He wanted it so often. Several times a day usually. It was easy enough to block him out since he preferred to penetrate me from behind. I never really had to look at him much. I just envisioned some sexy butch riding me and I was able to come quickly enough. God knows Enrico didn't leave me much time to get aroused at my normal pace. I either had to act as a brief, passive receptacle for his ejaculation or go somewhere in my head that was really hot."

"And that would be having sex with a woman?"

"Yes, mainly you. Since the day we met."

I put my fork down and peered in her direction. "You mean that all this time I've been fantasizing about you, you've been fantasizing about me while having sex with Enrico?"

Marie nodded and bowed her head. "I know it's awful."

I reached over and lifted her chin so I could look her in the eyes. "What's awful is that in a time of weakness, you made a really big mistake, and you've been paying for it ever since. It's time to stop paying for that mistake and make it right the best you can."

Marie looked at me with pleading in her eyes. "But how exactly do I accomplish that?"

"You admit that you made a mistake and work to undo that mistake, legally and whatever other way you need. Then you get back to living your life the way you want to live it. I hope I'll figure into that picture, but I don't want to be presumptuous. I mean, in a way, we hardly know each other. But I'm willing to rectify that."

She smiled back at me sadly. "I'd like for us both to rectify it, but I don't want to put you in harm's way. I've been wondering if I shouldn't go to that woman's shelter for a while to see if I can think things through."

I gulped back my fear of losing Marie and said bravely, "If that's what you need to do to help yourself, then I will support that decision. Just please don't make it based on some misplaced urge to protect me. I'll be fine. Enrico isn't going to harm me."

"You say that so easily, Jill, but I'm not so sure. Not after what I saw him do to my possessions. I don't even know if I will have any clothes left if I try to get back there for them."

"Listen. Let's take this one step at a time. Maybe you and Mack can go back to the house when you know Enrico is at work. You go in and get however many clothes you can pack quickly, and then get the hell out. I have some suitcases you can borrow so you'll have more space for stuff you want. We could also get some boxes at the liquor store. The sooner you do this, the better, I think. You don't want to give him time to realize that you're going to need more clothes. If he hasn't already destroyed them, you certainly don't want to give him time to dump them some place."

Marie nodded and began picking at her food again. "Maybe we could go tomorrow during my lunch hour. Enrico goes to work early, but he wouldn't be home yet. But that way I won't have to miss more work."

"Okay, I'll call Linda and have her arrange it with Mack for tomorrow if possible. Then we'll see about getting your life back on track."

Marie nodded again and went back to eating, albeit half-heartedly.

After we got our leftovers put in take-out containers, we headed for home.

Chapter 11
Home Sweet Disaster

When we got back home, I got Jolly into the house for dinner and some cuddles. Then I called Linda to set up the clothing heist with Mack, while Marie did the pregnancy test. We both breathed a sigh of relief when it came out negative. While I thought she would make a great mother, I also thought it might be a bit too much to add to Marie's current burden of wrenching her life back not only from Enrico, but also from her controlling mother. A baby would have complicated both of those situations greatly.

Later we headed to Southcenter Mall to buy some underclothes and an outfit for Marie to wear the next day until she was able to rescue her own clothes from her house. I kept looking over my shoulder, half expecting Enrico to pop up somewhere and accost us. I caught Marie looking around every few minutes too. I wondered if she were feeling as uneasy as I was. I wasn't sure what we were going to do about this predicament, but we certainly couldn't spend the rest of our lives watching our backs. Once when I was glancing around, I realized that Mack was standing only about twenty feet away from us. I breathed a prayer of thanks when I saw him. I nodded to him, and he smiled ever so slightly at me. I hadn't realized that he would actually be following us around town. Perhaps I should get his cell phone number in order to keep him apprised of our comings and goings.

Once we were home, Marie went and tried on her new outfit for me. She came out and did a quick spin. Her black flowery skirt twirled quite nicely when she turned like that. I applauded and Marie tossed a beautiful smile in my direction before leaving the room again. Having never been a girly girl, I wondered what it felt like to twirl around like that. About the time I decided that I could spend the rest of my life not knowing, Marie returned wearing the sweat pants and T-shirt I had set out for her to wear around the house until we could get her clothes back. I smiled and shook my head.

"What are you smiling about, Miss Jill?"

"I was just thinking about how absolutely adorable you look in your slightly too big T-shirt and your way too long sweat pants. The way the legs bag, you look like a pirate or something."

In answer, she leaned over to whisper in Jolly's ear. Jolly then ran over and leaped up to lick my face.

"You told her to do that?" I laughed.

Marie smiled coyly. "I told her you needed a good licking for that. Of course, she took it to mean that she needed to go over and lick your face, but I had another kind of licking in mind, since I was planning on doing the licking."

I petted Jolly's head, which made her tail wagging increase exponentially. "Perhaps she thinks I've had enough of your kind of licking for the time being, since we were at it so long last night."

"Tsk. I think not, but perhaps I'll have mercy on you for one night."

"Ah, well, we can always negotiate that later, once we get in bed for the night. You are going to sleep with me tonight, aren't you?"

"Yes, Jillie, I'll sleep with you. I'm sorry I was being so weird last night. It's just that I have so many conflicted emotions right now, but what you said at dinner really hit home. About paying for a mistake I'd made while I was feeling really hurt by Theresa. It's true. I felt as though Enrico was the best consolation prize at the time, and he came with the bonus of appeasing my mother. The only problem was that I was utterly unhappy about the whole arrangement, and it took the situation with you blowing up in my face to make me realize just how miserable I was. I'm sorry if I caused you grief the past couple days."

"Hey, it's okay. We'll just take everything nice and slow. You're welcome to stay here forever, but I'll understand if you need time to figure out what you want for your life."

"I don't need time to figure that out. I realize that I don't know you very well, Jill, but I do know that I care a great deal for you. I also know that I am very attracted to you. I'm willing to go from there, and if my mother doesn't like it, well then she just won't like it. She can just miss out on having her youngest child in her life. If her love is that conditional, she can just keep it. It really hurts to think that she might choose to do that, but I know I will always have Daddy's love at least. I know my brothers love me. I don't know what my sister thinks about me, but I guess she doesn't have time to think about anyone else anyway. She has her hands full with three kids and no husband. She knows about my past and yet has never said anything about it."

I patted the seat cushion on the couch next to me. "Come sit by me for a minute."

When she sat down tentatively, I put my arm around her shoulders and leaned back against the couch cushions, drawing her back with me. "If you want to grab any of your other belongings tomorrow, please do so. Pictures, whatever. I want you to feel at home here."

Marie started crying into my shoulder. "Thank you, Jill, but I don't think there's much left after Enrico's tantrum. I'll grab whatever he hasn't destroyed, if we have time. I just don't know what to expect when I go in there."

"Do you want me to come with you to help?"

She sat up abruptly. "No, I don't want you anywhere near there. I don't want to take any chances of running into Enrico when you're around."

I pulled her back against me again. "Okay, I'll stay at work and eat my lunch like a good girl. Until we get that restraining order, I really don't want to go out by myself, to tell you the truth. Since he knows where I work and what I look like, it wouldn't be hard for him to follow me somewhere and confront me. How about I make us both a tuna salad sandwich for lunch tomorrow? Then you can take yours with you when Mack drives you to your place, and I can eat mine in my office, where I'm surrounded by co-workers."

I felt Marie nod against my shoulder, so I took that as an affirmative to the tuna salad. I leaned up and let her rest her head against the couch cushions. "Okay then, I'll go make the sandwiches, so we can get ready for bed."

Marie got up and went into the bathroom, while I made our lunches for the next day. When I was done, I headed for the bedroom, followed by one tired Cocker Spaniel. I had to wonder at her fatigue. Surely she at least had gotten to catch up on her sleep today while we were at work. Perhaps her canine body was absorbing the stress that was emanating from our human bodies. I'd have to make sure I took her for a walk at the park soon. I knew she got plenty of exercise in the backyard, but it was my habit to take her to the park to play a couple times a week. I decided to schedule her grooming for this week too, even though it would be a little early. She probably needed that extra care during a time like this.

We didn't make love that night, but we did hold each other's naked body all through the night. Somehow that felt just as sexy as the wild sex from the night before. I woke up several times in the night to find us snuggled up together with a very contented dog at our feet.

The next morning we got up and took turns in the shower. Marie dressed in her black twirly skirt and the colorful flower print top she had bought that nicely contrasted with it. I wore my olive chinos with a navy polo shirt. Feeling very much at peace with the world, I set about making a nice breakfast of French toast with butter and real maple syrup. Marie shook her head as she entered the kitchen.

"What?"

"Jill, you sure know how to spoil a girl. I could get used to having someone cook for me."

"Ha! You'll soon see that my repertoire is rather limited, but I don't mind cooking what I know how to cook. The rest of the time, I just fake it or eat some frozen meal of a fairly healthy kind."

"I'll have to make dinner for you soon. I'm a pretty good cook, although I really don't like cooking all the time."

"We can just divide up the cooking and cleaning then. I'm used to doing it all anyway, so having any relief from it will be nice."

Marie smiled. "Me too. That's why it's such a nice change to have my meals handed to me when I walk into the room. That's something I haven't experienced since I left my parents' house."

I smirked. "Yeah, well, don't get too used to it. I'll hold you to that promise of cooking a meal for me. I'd love to have a night off now and again." I kissed the top of her head, while handing her a plate of French toast.

I lifted the latch on the doggy door so Jolly could go outside and run around a bit this morning. I usually left the doggy door open all day so she could come and go as she pleased, since the backyard was fully fenced. But I never really knew whether she went out while I was gone. She always came in before I left for work, and she was always waiting for me inside when I opened the door each evening. Even on the rare occasions when I drove back home for lunch, she'd be waiting at the door for me. I didn't know whether she just heard my car and came inside, or whether she came inside and stayed there until I got back home again. On rainy days, I never came home to muddy paw prints on the floor, so I knew she didn't go out on wet days. For that matter, I could hardly blame her, but I was a little surprised to think that she might just stay in every day until I returned home from work. Short of installing a camera inside the house, I realized that I'd probably never know the answer to that mystery.

As I stood there looking out the window, watching Jolly do her morning routine, I slipped into an altered state of consciousness and wasn't aware of Marie's quiet presence behind me.

"Jill? Where did you go?"

I started. "Oh! Sorry. I was just watching Jolly and wondering what she does all day while I'm gone."

"She probably sleeps most of the day while you're gone."

"Yeah, she probably didn't really need for me to install the doggy door, but at least I know that she can get out in the event of a fire or if I'm really late getting home at night. That makes me feel better at any rate. I don't know if it has helped her at all or not."

"She appreciates the gesture, no doubt. She's a sweet dog, Jill. She suits you well. Very affectionate and gentle spirited. She's pretty low key for a Cocker Spaniel really. Every other Cocker Spaniel I've known jumped up and down for hours at a time."

"So I've heard. She did that when she was a puppy, but by the time she was two, she'd mellowed out considerably."

"Maybe that's because you're so mellow. Maybe she realized that she doesn't need to be hyper to get attention from you because you're so attentive to her."

I shrugged. "I don't know." Just then, Jolly came back in through the canine entrance. I glanced up at the clock. "Yup, right on time. Are you ready to go?"

Marie nodded. "Does Jolly always come in just before you leave for work?"

"Yep. It's not like I trained her to do it either. She just knows when I leave for the day, so she comes in a couple minutes beforehand to say goodbye. I always know when it's time to go to work, that's for sure. So I guess in a way, I do have a watchdog."

Marie shook her head at me. "That was terrible."

I shrugged again. "Sorry."

We headed out the door for what should've been a normal day of work. Yet I felt an impending sense of doom, knowing that Marie was going to her house at lunchtime to pick up her clothes. I hoped she'd have some clothes to pick up. I prayed that Enrico would be nowhere around.

The morning flew by for me. I felt like the phone was going to have to be surgically removed from my left ear by the time the clock let me know that I was free to grab a bite to eat. I dug out my tuna salad sandwich and laid it on my desk. I scratched my head and rolled my chair back and forth a couple times. This sandwich was looking decidedly boring, so I jumped up and strolled to the vending machine for something to liven up my lunch hour. I bought a can of Dr. Pepper for a little pick me up and a bag of Cheetos to turn my fingers orange then headed back in the direction of my office. Just as I got to the door, I caught a glimpse of Marie's retreating figure heading out the back door towards the parking lot. I craned my neck to see in front of her. Sure enough, Mack had come to collect her. His tall, bulky figure utterly dwarfed my girlfriend in her twirly skirt. *Damn, her cute little ass sure looks good in that skirt.*

I resumed my mission of eating lunch. I managed to have the foresight to dig out a couple napkins from my desk drawer before I turned my fingers orange. Nothing worse than having orange Cheetos stains on your drawer pulls. Okay, so maybe there were a few things I could think of that would be worse, but for the time being, that was all I was worried about. Well, that and my cute girlfriend returning to the lion's den, hopefully while the lion was well away from the perimeter.

I tried to think about anything and everything except what she was doing at the moment. I didn't want to worry. I tried tossing Cheetos in the air and catching them in my mouth. The only problem with that was that it was getting orange crumbs all over my desk. Just when I'd decided to do only one more, I tossed it up into the air then noticed out of the corner of my eye that Mr. Watanabe was walking by. I immediately stopped what I was doing only to have the Cheeto come down and hit me on the nose. I glanced up and saw Mr. Watanabe standing in the doorway with his head cocked to one side. He smiled and winked at me then walked on down the hall.

I smiled back, stupidly no doubt, and took a bite of my sandwich. Nothing quite like making a fool of yourself in front of your boss. I seemed to do that a lot. I popped the top on my Dr. Pepper and guzzled down a few swallows. *Blech! This stuff tastes so much better over ice.* I paused to burp for a moment then decided to check my email during my lunch break. I hadn't turned on my computer at home for the past couple nights. I had been decidedly too busy to care about email. As soon as the email screen came on, I noticed a message from Linda. *Why on earth is she emailing me?*

The email was from this morning. She said that she'd tried to call me at home, but the phone just kept ringing, so I must've been on my way to work. She was letting me know that the restraining order was now in effect. I breathed a sigh of relief and decided to let Mr. Watanabe know the news as soon as I was finished with lunch. I deleted the batch of spam sitting in my junk mail box and signed out.

About that time, Mr. Watanabe came sauntering back past my office. He stopped, knocked on my door, and then launched a piece of popcorn in the air. It hit me square on the nose right where the Cheeto had landed. I looked up in surprise as he tossed another one, this one straight into the air. It came down nicely into his gaping mouth. He smiled again and continued on his way back to his office.

I shook my head and laughed. That was a totally cool thing for him to do. What a guy. I guess I hadn't made a complete fool out of myself after all. Or if I had, he was letting me know that he was a kid at heart and perfectly capable of doing silly things on his lunch breaks too. His actions reminded me of something my father would have done with me. I was one lucky woman to have a cool dad sort of a guy for a boss.

Suddenly I remembered about the restraining order. I quickly cleaned up the rest of the crumbs from my lunch and tossed everything in the trashcan underneath my desk. As I was checking the mirror to see if all my hairs were in place, it dawned on me that my telephone shouldn't have kept ringing without my answering machine picking up. *Maybe she forgot and called the old number.*

When I was convinced that I looked presentable and free of orange crumbs or crappy stuff in my teeth, I headed out to talk to my boss. His office door was wide open, so I poked my head in to find him tipping the nearly empty bag of popcorn crumbs into his mouth. He caught sight of me and lowered the bag, waving me in with his free hand. He crumpled the bag into a ball and tossed it into his trashcan behind his desk. For the first time, I noticed that he had a mini basketball hoop hooked on the side of his trash receptacle. He must've seen me notice it because he smiled, shyly almost, and said, "Big fan of basketball."

"Oh, did you ever play?"

He shook his head vehemently. "No, no. Too short."

"Me too, though I still used to shoot hoops with friends. Just never could make the team because I didn't have the speed and strength to make up for what I lacked in height."

He cleared his throat and tried to regain an ounce of decorum. "So, Ms. Michaels, what can I do for you today? I assume you aren't here to talk about basketball."

I nodded and sat on the edge of the chair in front of his desk, so as not to be standing over him. "I, uh, I just wanted to let you know that I got a message from a friend of mine who is helping Marie. She says that the restraining order is now active, so if Enrico appears on this site, we are now allowed to call the police immediately. I gather that you will soon receive a copy of the paperwork via courier service."

He nodded several times as though digesting important information. "This is good. Ms. Garcia is in a better position now. How is she doing?"

"She's good. I mean, you know, considering the circumstances. She's over at her house collecting her clothes and personal belongings during her lunch break." When a look of alarm crossed his features, I hastened to add, "With a very big and scary bodyguard, of course."

"Good, good." His face relaxed visibly.

When I realized that I didn't have anything else to add, I rose to head back to my office. As I did so, Mr. Watanabe cleared his throat again. I glanced in his direction and noticed a small smile on his face.

"Is there something else you wanted to know?"

If he weren't my boss, I would have sworn that the slightest of blushes suddenly colored his cheeks. I suddenly saw the little boy that he must have been several decades ago.

"I was merely wondering if you had caught most of the Cheetos on your nose or in your mouth."

I burst out laughing. I couldn't help it. The look on his face coupled with the question let me know that I had found a kindred spirit in my boss. There was a real person behind the suit. I knew we had crossed a threshold in that moment. I finally stopped laughing and said, "actually the one you saw hit my nose was the only one. The rest went into my mouth or sadly enough onto the floor or my desk." I quickly added, "I cleaned up the mess, of course."

He smiled, stood up, and reached out his hand to me. "Thank you again for coming to see me, Ms. Michaels. My encounters with you are always pleasant and most entertaining. You remind me of my youngest daughter. She too is what you call a tomboy. I had no sons, so she was the one who went to all the ballgames with her father." He winked again and put another fatherly hand over the one already in his grasp.

Then he released me and I spun around to leave. "Thank you, sir. The feeling is mutual. Er, except the part about your daughter, of course." I shook my head and grinned at him. When I headed back to my office, I nearly plowed into my friend Dave along the way. "Dave, sorry, I didn't see you."

The former college linebacker shouldered me playfully. "Yeah, well, I'm pretty hard to miss, you know."

"One would think. Selling lots of cars out there?"

"Always, but Hondas mostly sell themselves. I'm just there to hammer out the terms of the deal. Gotta get back though before I'm late. Catcha later."

"Yeah, have fun."

He took off in the direction of the sales area, while I headed the opposite direction towards the parts department. I heard the phone ringing again when I got close to the door of my office. When I answered the phone, there was a slight pause and then a click. I looked at the phone in my hand. I didn't get wrong numbers generally because the call had to be routed through the main office, which then directed calls about parts directly to me. I had an adrenaline rush as I thought about Enrico's call earlier that week. He certainly knew where to find me most of the time. I suddenly felt rather vulnerable in my office away from most of the other employees. I decided to close the door, something I rarely did. It seemed to be the only thing that stood between me and anyone who might be lurking in the building.

I sat down at my desk and checked for messages that had been left during my absence. Engrossed in my work at the computer, I felt rather than heard someone's presence on the other side of the door. I looked up suddenly and froze, waiting to see who was coming into the sanctuary of my office. I was relieved to see Marie's lovely face. "Hey, you're back. How did it go?"

She smiled warmly as she stepped into the room, closing the door behind her. "Pretty well, considering he hasn't cleaned up the new mess he made since I left. I don't know what he's planning to use for dishes now that he's broken everything in the kitchen cupboards. At least he hadn't gotten as far as my clothes closet yet, though no doubt he would've gotten there eventually."

"So you have clothes again?" I smiled at her, glad that she wouldn't have the added expense of a new wardrobe.

"Yes, I got every last stitch of clothing I own out of there, including the ones in the laundry room, waiting to be washed. I hope you don't mind if I wash some clothes tonight."

I shook my head, glad to know that there'd be a tonight. I still wasn't sure what she was going to decide to do with her future. It was best to take it day by day, while making it clear that she was welcome to stay with me as long as she liked or forever, whichever came first. "No problem. I have a heavy-duty washing machine and dryer in the utility room off the kitchen. I think they're both available at the moment."

"Thanks. I'd better get to work then. I just wanted to let you know I had gotten back safely."

"Thank you, Marie. I really appreciate that. I've been trying not to worry about you. I knew you had Mack with you, but I still didn't want a confrontation. Oh, by the way, the restraining order went through. I let Mr. Watanabe know so he can inform security. You'll get the paperwork soon, no doubt. I think Linda said that she was sending a courier over here with copies for everyone."

"Good, I'm so relieved. That will help a little bit."

I nodded, thinking about the phone call that wasn't really a phone call.

"What is it, Jill? You look worried."

I shrugged. "It's probably nothing, but I had a hang-up call this afternoon, which is something I rarely get since the receptionist routes calls that are only from people requesting the parts department."

"Do you think it was Enrico?"

"I really don't know who it was since there was no one on the line talking to me."

She furrowed her brows in thought for a moment. "Well, I guess it's best not to give it too much thought for the time being."

I nodded, trying to seem more confident and assured than I was feeling at the moment.

She headed out the door and back to work, so I turned my attention to the computer screen. When the phone rang an hour later, I jumped. I picked it up quickly and tried to sound normal. "Parts department, Jill speaking."

"Is this the Jill Michaels who lives on SE 166th Street?"

I hung up. *Shit! How did Enrico find out where I live?*

I put a call into Linda, who gave me Mack's cell phone number. I called him immediately and told him what had happened. "How did he find out my address, Mack? I've always had an unlisted and unpublished phone number."

Mack's deep, gravelly voiced answered, "Do you have access to the Internet right now?"

"Yes."

"Google your phone number."

"What?"

"You heard me. Just do it. You do know how to do a Google search, don't you?"

"Yes." I maneuvered my way to the Google search page and entered my home phone number. "Oh, my gawd. There's my information. How can they do that when my phone number is unlisted and supposedly unpublished?"

"That only covers what the phone company does with your information. It doesn't cover other contingencies."

"Like the Internet?"

"Yeah, like the Internet. But there is a way to block that. If you look at your screen carefully, you'll see that. Of course, it's too late as far as Enrico is concerned, but still well worth doing now."

"Thanks. I just clicked the button to block that info. So now what happens?"

"So now I go back and sit at your house as usual and wait for the guy to show his face. I have plenty of friends on the police force still. I'll call in today to see if I can get some extra patrols for your area. We'll nail this guy, Jill. He's already tipped his hand. He might think he's clever for tracking you down, but he was pretty stupid to let you know that he'd found you. I think he wants to play cat and mouse games with you, but he's going to be the one who winds up being the mouse, and I've got lots of mousetraps for losers like him. Don't worry about anything. Just stay home tonight once you get home, okay? I'm going to head over there now and check on things."

"Um, okay, but watch out for my dog."

"You have a watchdog?"

"Now why does everyone assume that my dog is a watchdog? I didn't say that, though Jolly probably would watch you all right, from the comfort of the sofa."

Mack's chuckle was more like a subsonic rumble. "Jolly? Doesn't sound too ferocious."

"Nope. Smart though. She can probably spell and define *ferocious*, but don't ask her to act it. She's not a good actress. She's just Jolly. Her name says it all."

"Okay, then, I'll beware of the jolly dog. If everything's all right, I'll come back here and follow you ladies home, if you don't mind."

"Mack, I wouldn't mind if you moved in with us."

He rumbled again. "I know about fifty guys who would jump all over that, but I'll be a gentleman for Linda's sake."

I smiled despite myself. "Thank you, Mack. Thanks for being there for us. Hopefully this won't take long. Maybe he'll show up tonight so we can be done with him. Then you can go back home to…"

"A six-pack and reruns on the tube? I'm not missing out on much. Now if baseball season was in full swing, then it would be another matter."

"Yes, well, let's get this over before that starts up."

"Jill, can I get your cell phone number so I can call if anything weird is going on at your place? If there is anything amiss, I want you to go to the Renton Police Department and ask for Sam Keaton. Okay?"

I scribbled down the name and nodded my head, hoping he could hear my marbles rolling around in there. "Okay, got it." I gave him my number and we hung up.

I glanced up at the clock. We still had an hour to go before we could call it a day, so I went back to my computer project but before I could get anything accomplished, the telephone starting ringing nonstop again. It was funny how it always seemed to come in waves. It was as though everyone in King County needed parts for their cars all at the same time. *Do cars in King County all break down in unison?*

When it was finally time to leave, I cleared my desk and headed out to meet Marie. She agreed to meet me outside her office door. Everyone was in agreement that she should not be out in public alone for the time being. I wondered how many days of that would be required. I couldn't help wondering if she felt like a criminal, having to be escorted everywhere she went. I asked her that on the ride home.

"You know, Jill, I haven't given it a moment's thought. I don't want to be alone right now. Enrico really scared me when he started throwing everything around the house. My father is a gentle man. I don't think I heard him raise his voice even one time."

"That's the part I don't get, Marie. People are usually attracted to people who are like their parents. You should've been attracted to someone who is more like your father."

"Actually, Jill, Enrico is more like my mother. She is the loud one in our family. Angry too sometimes, which is why I think my father tried to be a source of quiet strength and gentle caring. You are more like him."

"Gosh, thanks, Marie. I like the sound of that."

"Mr. Watanabe reminds me of my father too."

"Yeah, mine too. Speaking of Mr. Watanabe, I've got to tell you what he did today."

I proceeded to tell Marie about my interactions with our boss today. As we neared my house, Marie and I were in hysterics, laughing about it. When we turned the final corner, I realized immediately that something had gone terribly wrong. There were police cars all up and down the street on both sides of the road, lights flashing, nearly blocking the throughway. I drove slowly up to my house and into my driveway unable to process the scene before me. The front window of my house had been shattered, and Marie's car was obviously totaled with all the damage it had sustained being driven straight through it. The blue tarp that had covered it was lying in the yard next to the carport, one corner of it flapping slightly in the breeze.

Marie and I both just sat there with our mouths hanging open. My mind flashed on the famous Edvard Munch painting, "The Scream." In that moment, that was how I felt, like I was screaming, but no sound was coming from my mouth. I glanced at Marie and wondered if she were feeling the same way. I reached over and touched her hand.

Just then Mack was at my car window gently tapping on it. "Jill, I've been trying to call your cell phone. Don't you have it with you?"

"What?" I rolled down my window.

"Your cell phone? I've been calling your number nonstop for the past half hour."

"Oh, it's here." I reached in my jacket pocket, pulled it out, and flipped it open. "Um, but it looks as though I needed to recharge it. Shit!"

"That's the least of your worries right now, I suspect." He opened my car door so I could get out then he went around and opened the door for Marie. "God, I don't know where to begin, ladies. So much has happened." He ran a beefy hand over his crew-cut and released a huge sigh.

I cleared my throat. "Well, I'm just guessing here, but I'd say that Enrico paid us a visit."

Mack looked at me and laughed ever so slightly. "Yeah, I guess you could say that. The bad news you can see for yourself. The good news, sort of, is that he won't be back again to bother you."

I glanced at Marie then back at Mack. "He's in jail then?"

Mack put his hands on his hips and looked down at the ground. "Not exactly." Then he turned to Marie and put his hands on both of her shoulders. "Marie, I'm sorry to have to tell you this, but Enrico was killed when he drove your car through the front of the house."

Marie peered at him and shook her head slightly, almost as though she didn't quite hear him. She looked dazed to say the least. "What did you say?"

"Your husband is dead, Mrs. Garcia. The ambulance took him to the hospital about fifteen minutes ago."

"What? How? I don't understand any of this. How did he know where Jill lived?"

Mack looked at me puzzled. "You didn't tell her that Enrico had gotten your address?"

I scratched my head. "I, no, I guess I didn't. I didn't want to scare her, and I knew you were going to go to my house to check on things. When I didn't hear anything, I just figured everything was okay. God, I'm sorry. I didn't realize that my phone charge was so low."

Mack shook his head once. "Hey, Jill, it's okay. Shit happens. In this case, a lot of shit happened at once."

I let out a blast of air that I had been holding inside for too long. "Yeah, so it seems." Suddenly my thoughts went to Jolly. "Oh my god! Where's my dog?"

Mack quickly reassured me that she was fine. Apparently she had been outside barking at Enrico when he was breaking into Marie's car. She must have been clear of the house when the collision sent glass flying everywhere. When Mack got there, he had tied her up around back to keep her from returning to the house and getting cut.

Just then a policeman walked up to us. He looked in my direction. "You the owner?"

I nodded then added, "Of the house, but not the car."

"Right, we already know about the car."

I squinted in the direction of the police officer. "When did all this happen?"

"About an hour ago. One of your neighbors actually witnessed it because he was looking out the window to find out why your dog was barking like crazy. Apparently he works nights and sleeps in the daytime, and he'd never heard him bark before, so he figured something must be wrong."

I nodded, mentally correcting the gender switch of my canine companion.

He continued. "I need to ask you a few questions for the police report. You might want to call your insurance company as soon as we're done here."

I nodded again and sort of zoned out, looking at Marie standing there, unseeing, just leaning against Mack's chest. It looked to me as though she had checked out and not left a forwarding address. I answered the officer's questions with one part of my brain while another part of my brain picked up on Jolly's barking in the backyard. I knew she was as anxious as I was for our happy reunion to begin. She must have been scared with all that noise. Normally this is a pretty quiet neighborhood.

I wondered if Enrico had been drunk when he'd done this. As though she had read my mind, or I had read hers, Marie looked up at Mack and asked him that very question. Mack confirmed that he had reeked of alcohol, but they wouldn't know how far over the legal limit he had been until the autopsy report came back.

A tow truck pulled up to haul Marie's car out of the window. I interrupted the policeman and told them to hold off for a minute, since we both needed to call our insurance companies. Mack handed me his cell phone, while I fumbled through my wallet, looking for my insurance card. I was hoping that State Farm was ready and waiting to be a good neighbor to me, since that was their motto. Before I'd finished answering the policeman's questions, my agent was driving up to take a look at the damage. Camera in hand, she took several pictures of the outside. I handed her the keys so she could get inside without having to crawl over the car hanging out of my front window.

After everything was wrapped up with the police officer, I followed my insurance agent inside. I answered what questions I could then she went to talk to the policeman. Then Marie's insurance agent showed up to look at the damage to her car and my house. The two agents conferred and agreed that Marie's insurance company would be the one settling the claim for my house and her car, since it was pretty obvious that my house hadn't reached out, grabbed the car, and thrown it through its own front window like a hungry troll gobbling a Honda snack.

When all that was settled, the tow truck pulled Marie's car out. Her agent snapped several photos and authorized them to take the car away after Marie had a few minutes to retrieve personal items. She waved them off without even looking inside the car. As it was dragged away, she stood looking up the street at its pathetic form. "That is the nicest car I've ever owned." She was clearly in shock. Her insurance agent assured her that she'd be able to replace it with an equally nice new one.

It was stupid, but my first thought was, *Too bad you can't sue the bastard who did this.* I also found myself wishing that I had a magic wand that could wave all these people and this mess into another dimension. *How did my life get so complicated suddenly? And noisy. God, it's noisy.*

Chapter 12
Shattered Dreams

Mack came inside with us after the police left. He called a couple buddies of his to bring plywood to board up the front window until it could be fixed. While Enrico had destroyed the window and its frame pretty thoroughly, the low wall beneath it appeared to be sound.

Mack also called Linda, who vowed to come over right away, saying that she was on her way out the door anyway.

Marie told me that she needed to be by herself for a little while, so she went into the bedroom and closed the door behind her. I motioned for Mack to sit on a kitchen chair, since relaxing in the living room was a bit out of the question at the moment. I went out the back door to greet Jolly and let her know that everything was going to be all right and that she had been a very good watchdog. I explained that I needed to clean up the mess in the living room, so she would have to stay outside for a while longer. I untied the rope around her collar so she could romp around the yard freely. I slid the doggy door shut when I came in, so Jolly wouldn't come in and surprise me.

Then I set out to clean up the mess. I had grabbed a big trashcan from the backyard and brought it into the house with me. I put a thick plastic trash bag in it. The biggest pieces of glass Mack laid carefully to one side, while I swept and scooped up several thousand shards of glass from the living room and kitchen floors and dumped them into the garbage can. Realizing I'd never get all this done without some serious help, I checked the phone book and called several housecleaning companies until I got one that could send a couple people over immediately to help set things right. I kept sweeping and scooping, while Mack kept stacking the big hunks. I paused to get a box for all the big pieces. I figured that I could take all this glass to work and put it in the dumpster there. That would be safer than having the garbage people handle it.

The cleaning help arrived the same time as Linda. I gave them instructions to start vacuuming the couch cushions and all the nooks and crannies of my living room, so I could let my dog run freely through here without worrying that she'd cut her paws on a stray piece of glass. They got busy while Mack, Linda, and I moved out to the backyard to talk.

Linda looked at me with grave concern etched in her features. "How is Marie?"

I shook my head. "I don't know really. Deep in shock, I think. The guy may have been a loser, but he was still her husband. I can't even imagine what thoughts are running through her head right now. She's in the bedroom there, if you want to go talk with her."

Linda nodded, hugged me, and then went into the house to see Marie.

I looked at Mack. "You're all right, you know. I don't know what we would've done without you the past couple days. It's a shame you and Linda aren't still together. We could double date or something, you know, after we've all recovered from this fiasco."

Mack laughed and shook his head. "Well, thanks, you're all right yourself. I didn't know what to expect from this lesbian friend of Linda's that she talked about all the time."

"Ah, come on. She doesn't talk about me that much surely. We've hardly even seen each other this past year."

"Maybe I should have said who talked about you at odd moments."

"What do you mean?"

"Like the first time she mentioned you, we had just finished having sex. That struck me as rather odd, let me tell you. Made me feel just a little insecure. Then when it became apparent that the physical aspect of our relationship just wasn't happening, I thought about that again and called her on it. She blew it off as nothing, of course, but I'm not convinced that she's not carrying a torch for you."

"Please, Mack, you've got to be kidding me. She always seemed so, um, well, straight in college. More than straight, she seemed downright uptight sometimes about sexuality. She had been married and divorced once already, which really puzzled me, because she never talked about it. I never asked about it. I just figured that it was her business and that maybe she wanted to forget about it. There was never any indication there that she might prefer women to men, just that she'd had a bad first marriage."

"Yeah, well, I think that might have been lack of opportunity rather than lack of interest."

"Hunh. Maybe she's just finding that out about herself. Or she could just be curious, since she does have a lesbian friend. I think a lot of women with lesbian friends get curious about what it would be like. It doesn't necessarily mean that they want to switch teams, you know."

Mack pushed his lips out like he was trying not to laugh.

"What? What's so damn funny?"

He shook his head a couple times. "Nothing. I'm just seeing why Linda finds you so 'charming,' I believe was the word she used. No, no, it was 'tomboyish charm.'"

I punched him in the bicep. "Now, stop! You're embarrassing me."

Just then Linda joined us at the back of the house. She called to me from the steps. "If you don't like my bodyguard, could you at least not damage him? I might have need of him again some time."

I walked over to her, while Mack stayed behind and petted a very friendly and happy dog who had jumped up to get his attention. "Sorry about beating on your bodyguard. We were just about to start arm wrestling to see who got to bed you for the night."

Linda blushed a deep shade of red. "I see. You are kidding, aren't you?"

I smiled. "Yes, Linda, I'm kidding. I wouldn't stand a chance against him anyway, now would I?"

"Now as far as I'm concerned there need not be an arm wrestling match. Why not just let me choose between you?" She leered at me rather lustfully, which made me realize that there might be a grain of truth to what Mack was saying.

"Ha! Ha! You're such a kidder. Seriously though, how's Marie doing in there?"

Linda's face sobered quickly. "She's really torn up and can't quite decide which emotion to express first. She's mad as hell at Enrico for doing what he did to her car and your house. She's grief stricken for a man with whom she had, until quite recently, been trying to build a life. She's angry with her mother for pushing her to marry Enrico. She feels guilty for involving you in this. She's scared because she doesn't know what to do next. Glazed over the top of these emotional layers is a coat of shock that is not likely to wear off for a couple days. God help her when it does."

"Gosh, Linda, no need to sugarcoat. Please go ahead and speak frankly here."

She glared at me. "You know I never sugarcoat things. If you want the sugarcoated version of a situation, I'm afraid you're going to be sadly disappointed with me every time."

I reached up and hugged her neck. "I know, Linda. I'm just kidding." I wondered if Linda was really this upset about Marie, or if I'd hurt her feelings by blowing off the option of having sex with her.

"You're always just kidding. That's what's so maddening about you. No one knows when to take you seriously or when you're just kidding." She said the last two words quite sarcastically.

"Wow! I'm sorry, Linda. I didn't mean to offend you by trying to be lighthearted about this. I know there's nothing funny about it. I just try not to take everything so seriously."

"Well, maybe you should try to take a few things in life more seriously."

I started to ask for a couple examples of things that would benefit from a more dour approach but thought better of it. The present circumstances were example enough at the moment. I glanced in Mack's direction and somehow he must have heard my unspoken plea for help because he walked over to us and looked at me. "Well, my dear, I suspect that my job is done here now unless there's something else you need me to do to help you clean up this mess." He waited as though he really wanted me to answer him, so I figured it was a real offer of help. But I was pretty sure that the front flower garden and yard could wait until the weekend, and there were two people already cleaning away inside the house.

I sighed and ran my hands through my hair, causing it to spike up on top. "No, I'm good, and I don't know how to thank you for all you did already."

Mack smiled at my hairdo. "Well, how about we take in a Mariners game sometime this summer? You can supply the food and I'll supply the tickets."

"Dude, that sounds to me like you're doing the lion's share of treating."

He shook his head. "Nah, I get free tickets all the time, but Linda here doesn't like baseball."

"Oh, I never said that I didn't like baseball. I only said that I didn't get it."

"What's not to get?" I rubbed my chin, considering this.

"It's just that it seems like it takes so long for anything interesting to happen. Not like football, or soccer, as you Americans call it."

I put my hands on my hips and scowled in her direction. "Hey, you're an American citizen now, so you can't say 'you Americans' any more."

Mack laughed quietly in his rumbling way. "I think I'll leave you two ladies to battle this one out of your own. Let me know, if you ever need a bodyguard again. This has been a most interesting case. I'll let you know next time I get tickets to Safeco. Then we can all go and experience the boredom that is baseball together." He rumbled again and winked in my direction. He leaned over and kissed Linda on the cheek. "So long, and thanks for all the fish."

She smiled widely, kissed him on the cheek, and then hugged him for good measure. "Thanks again, Mack."

After he'd gone I turned to Linda, "Fish? What fish? Did I miss something there?"

She laughed. "It's an allusion to one of the Douglas Adams books in the science fiction series, *The Hitchhikers Guide to the Galaxy*. I read them to Mack, once upon a time."

"Oh, I've heard of those, but never read them."

"Well, you jolly well ought to read them. They're superbly and ridiculously silly, much like yourself. I think you'd like them. I would loan you my copy, but I never loan that particular book out, so you're on your own."

"Didn't they make a movie from that book?"

"Yes, but don't even think about renting it without reading the books first. It's absolutely criminal. You won't get half the jokes."

I held up my hands in surrender. "I promise. Listen, I need to get back inside to finish making the house safe for Jolly to come in for the evening. I also have to figure out what to do about dinner. I really need to go grocery shopping, but I was trying to wait until after I got paid tomorrow."

"I haven't eaten either. How about I make a run into town and pick up something at the deli at Fred Meyers? What do you think Marie might like from there?"

I shrugged. "No clue. We haven't really hung around together enough for me to know that. Most of the eating we've done together has been done during our lunch breaks at work, so we go to places that are near there. Why don't I just go and ask her? I'll be right back."

I knocked softly on the bedroom door, entering when I heard a sniffly "Come in."

"Hey, sweetheart. I realize that you may not be in the mood to eat at the moment, but Linda's going to run to Freddy's deli to pick up something for dinner. Is there anything in particular you want from there?"

She shook her head slightly.

I walked over and wrapped my arms around her. "I know there is nothing that I could say or do right now to make this all seem better, but I do want you to know that I'm here and that I love you and will honor whatever you need to do to take care of yourself."

Tears started streaming down her face, soaking into my shirt. After a minute or two, she said, "You're so good to me, even after all this."

I leaned back to try to look at her. "What do you mean after all this? You weren't the one who tried to park your car on my sofa. Don't even think about blaming yourself for Enrico's drunken behavior. I'm really sorry that he went out that way, but I guess he was just too far gone to know what he was doing. That is not your fault, so stop that nonsense right now. Do you hear me?"

Marie sniffed and wiped at her face with a tissue. "I know I didn't do it, but it happened because of me."

"No, Marie. It didn't happen because of you. It happened because of Enrico. We all choose how we're going to respond to difficult situations in our lives. Apparently going into a drunken rage was how Enrico chose to deal with your breakup, but that still doesn't make it your fault. Okay?"

She nodded slightly. I wasn't convinced that she had really released that sense of guilt and responsibility, but I figured that some counseling would help her get beyond that.

"So what about the deli? Is there anything you want? Barbecued chicken? Cole slaw? Mashed potatoes?"

She shook her head again. "I'm sorry, Jillie. I just can't think about food at the moment. I'll eat whatever you get, if I get hungry enough to eat at all. Right now, I'm not hungry."

I nodded, hugged her again, and then went back out to confer with Linda. I gave her my order for the night and had her get enough for two. I tried to pay her for it, but she wouldn't hear of it.

"No, love, I'll treat tonight. Goodness knows you have enough expenses to deal with at the present moment, though I'd think you should be able to recoup the cleaning expenses from the insurance agency. Be sure to get receipts from your hired people out there. You can just submit them to your own agent, I suspect, who will in turn give them to Marie's insurance agent for reimbursement. It may take a little while, but you should be able to get that back anyway."

I nodded and walked Linda to the door then turned to see how the glass extraction process was coming along. The clean up crew pronounced the living room area safe, if not repaired. They carried the demolished recliner out to the porch to await disposal. Not wanting to start a neighborhood trend of having broken down recliners on my front porch, I racked my brain trying to figure out how I could get the wreckage from today to the dumpsters at work. Then the light dawned brightly on my weary brain. *Ah, yes, good old Dave has a pickup he rarely uses.*

I paid the cleaners with a check that would be good first thing in the morning, thanks to automatic deposit. Then after I saw them out, I called Dave to see if I could borrow his pickup over the weekend to carry the glass and broken recliner pieces to their final, or nearly final, resting grounds. Thankfully he didn't ask too many questions, though I don't know who wouldn't be asking me questions tomorrow, once they read the morning news. I'd seen a television camera crew out there just before the tow truck hauled Marie's sad looking car out of my living room.

What truly puzzled me was how a drunken man could drive a car through a plate glass window so perfectly that he hadn't harmed the surrounding wall. I'd have to have it checked when the window got replaced, just to make sure it really was sound, but it certainly looked undamaged. That seemed like a miracle to me. I couldn't figure out how he'd gotten up enough speed to become airborne. That's the only way he could've cleared the little wall that held the window. I shook my head and decided to ask my neighbor about it in the next few days, while it would still be fresh in his memory.

Thinking about all the things I needed to do tomorrow, I decided to call Mr. Watanabe and let him know what happened. I knew he'd read the paper tomorrow and find out that Marie's car had been driven through my window. I didn't want him to worry unnecessarily. I figured that we should probably both take a personal day tomorrow anyway, since I needed to work with the insurance company to get my house fixed, and Marie needed to have some space for the time being. She would have to make arrangements for Enrico's remains, and I dreaded the thought of her having to do all of that stuff. She'd be able to take bereavement time, and I had plenty of personal time available. This seemed as though it would qualify as being personal.

I made the call to Mr. Watanabe. He was very understanding, of course, and assured me that Marie should take all the time she needed before she came back to work. I knew Candace would be pissed about Marie's absence, but she'd just have to get over herself. I also let him know that I was going to be putting some stuff in the dumpsters there to be picked up.

When I was finished with my phone call, I went to the doggie door and opened it so Jolly could get back inside. She must have heard the sound and come running because in seconds she was bowling me over in her exuberance. I sat on the kitchen floor and let her lick my face. I knew that she needed assurance that everything was okay, that I was okay. I praised her some more for going out and barking at the prowler. She almost seemed proud of herself. I was mostly grateful that she had been out of the way when Enrico had pulled his daredevil stunt.

Sitting on the kitchen floor with my face in Jolly's fur, I realized just how close we had all come to disaster. Even though Marie's car was demolished, at least we were all safe. A car could be replaced. The house could be repaired, but none of us are so fixable or replaceable. It was a shame Enrico had taken his own life in his drunken rage, but at least now Marie and I wouldn't always be looking over our shoulders for him. We could be done with him for good. I felt somewhat guilty at feeling so relieved that he was dead. It wasn't as though I had wanted him to die. I had only wanted him out of Marie's life so she could start over again. This had certainly been a nightmarish way to bring about those results.

I hugged Jolly closer to my chest and whispered that she was the best watchdog ever. She licked my face and wagged her tail some more.

When I looked up finally, Marie was standing at the edge of the kitchen, watching me with tears in her eyes. "I don't know what I would have done if anything bad had happened to Jolly. I'm so sorry about everything else, but that would've been the worst thing."

I nodded through my tears of joy and grief, tears that had begun to fall while I was hugging my precious canine companion. I'd had Jolly for only five years, but it felt more like my whole life. I'd gotten her not too long after I'd gotten out of college and discovered how worthless a degree in philosophy is when you don't plan to get your PhD so you can teach it. Right after I got her, I landed the job at Renton Honda, and even though it wasn't a glamorous job, it paid well enough to enable me to buy this house, with a little help from my parents, and build a life for myself and Jolly.

Just then there was a knock at the door, and I realized that Linda must be returning with dinner. I released Jolly and wiped my eyes quickly. Then I got up from the floor to open the door. I let Linda in, relieving her of some of the bags she was carrying. In that moment, I realized just how hungry I had gotten with all the cleaning, calling, and doggie cuddling. I got out plates and silverware for us to use. I put a piece of broiled chicken and a variety of vegetables on Marie's plate and then made mine. I piled on lots of mashed potatoes and gravy to go with my chicken and veggies. Linda fixed herself a plate, and we all sat down at the kitchen table to eat.

Before we began, Marie stopped us. "I don't normally do this, but I'd like to say grace before we eat."

Linda and I both nodded and bowed our heads.

Marie began to speak softly, "Whoever it is out there who kept Jill's dog from being harmed, I thank you. I thank you also for these two wonderful women who have helped me so much during this hard time in my life. And wherever Enrico is now, I ask the angels to take him to heaven and help him to get straightened out. I forgive him for what he did, and I hope he will forgive me too for how I hurt him. Amen."

When I looked up, both Linda and Marie had tears in their eyes. Linda whispered, "Amen."

Marie made a few valiant attempts at eating, but it was obvious that she was too upset to eat much. Eventually she put her fork down and just watched us eat, though I don't think she was actually seeing anything. She seemed to have retreated inside her pain again. I found myself praying to whoever had watched out for Jolly to watch out for Marie too and not let her get lost while she was in there. I caught Linda observing her with concern in her eyes.

Finally Linda put her fork down and reached across the table to touch Marie's hand. "I'm going to make some phone calls tomorrow and find a counselor for you to talk to about all this. You need someone besides Jill to help you make sense of what has just transpired in your life. I know you'll have other arrangements to make tomorrow regarding Enrico, so I'll see if I can make your appointment for midweek next week. Okay?"

Marie nodded her head. Apparently Linda's words had penetrated the curtain that hung in front of her features. "I guess I need to go home some time and clean the house. I can go back there now and not put you out any more, Jill."

I looked intently at her. "You can if you want to, Marie, but you're not putting me out by being here. You're welcome forever, if you'd like. It's totally up to you. I understand though if you want to go home. I can help you clean up the mess he made with your dishes. Maybe I can hire that service again to make light work of it. They were fast and, from the looks of the living room, thorough."

She nodded without looking at me.

I sighed and looked at Linda. She put her other hand over mine. "Well, girls, I think it's time I headed for home. I have two goldfish at home waiting for dinner. I mustn't keep them waiting any longer."

I looked at her and frowned. "Goldfish? Since when do you have goldfish?"

She smiled sardonically. "Since some well meaning client gave them to me as a thank you gift. She works in a pet store. It was a nice gesture, and I've actually grown quite attached to them. Well, not necessarily to this pair. This is my third pair. They don't seem to be all that keen on longevity. I don't know if I'm doing something wrong or whether they just don't hang around long. I've been meaning to get a book about them, but I haven't had time. I just keep naming each pair the same thing, so there's at least a sense of continuity."

I shook my head. "You never cease to amaze me with your hidden wonders." I laughed. "I'll have to come over and meet your goldfish some time."

"Do, Jill, love. Maybe we can go there before or after the infamous baseball game we're going to attend."

I grinned. "You're on. I'm going to make you live up to your promise to go to a Mariners game."

Marie looked at me with a puzzled expression. "You're going to a Mariners game?"

"Yeah, it was Mack's idea. I wanted to thank him for all he's done, so he made me promise to go with him next time he got free tickets. I have to provide all the food."

Marie teared up again.

I reached out quickly to touch Marie's hand. "What? What happened? Did I say something wrong?"

She shook her head slightly. "I'm sorry. It's just that Enrico had season passes for this year. You can have them.

I've never been, but he was going to make me go this year, or he was going to take one of his buddies if I wouldn't go. I definitely don't want to go now"

I put my hand on her back. "Okay, we can talk about that later. It isn't important right now."

I got up to walk Linda to her car. As we hugged, she made me promise not to let Marie go home alone the first time. I promised, knowing that she'd have to get a ride from me anyway, unless she planned to get a rental car until her insurance company paid out for her wrecked vehicle. It suddenly dawned on me that Enrico's car would have to be sitting somewhere near my house. Otherwise, how did he get here in the first place?

As Linda got in her car, I scanned the block for an old Chevy Nova. Sure enough. Three houses down was a car I didn't recognize as being a regular in the neighborhood. I guess Marie still had a car, though I didn't know if she would want to drive it. At least she could use it as a trade in.

I blew a kiss to Linda as she drove away. I stood there for a few moments watching her tail lights move up the road away from me. I couldn't help but wonder about the dynamics between Linda and Mack. They seemed rather couple-like, but mostly in a Platonic way now. They definitely didn't seem passionate towards one another. They were more like an old married couple that had decided that sex wasn't a necessity in their relationship any more for one reason or another. Which led me to the worrisome thought that Linda might truly be interested in a relationship with a woman, and one woman in particular, namely me.

It's not that I didn't find Linda attractive; it was just that I was so used to thinking about her in an older sister sort of way. Shifting gears now would be like trying to shift into reverse without clutching. The grinding sound was nearly headache-inducing, even though it was only imaginary. Plus now there was Marie in my life.

Once Linda's car had turned the corner, I headed back inside to check on Marie. She was a puzzle I wasn't sure I would ever solve. She was really fragile right now. I knew she was hurting because of Enrico. Her grief over him was complicated by her sense of culpability regarding her emotionally, and now physically, adulterous relationship with me. I pondered how a person was supposed to know when someone is truly no longer married. Is it when the couple gets the divorce decree? Is it when they've ceased having sex? Is it when one of the partners realizes it's time to move on, even though it may take a little while to enact that move? When is it okay to be with someone in a situation like this?

I could think of reasons why any of these times could be considered valid, but I could also think of exceptions to each potential gauge. For instance there are couples who have sex after getting their divorce decree—the infamous "farewell fuck." I'd experienced one or two of those in the past, even though I'd never been legally married. Some couples continue having sex and living together even though they no longer love each other, or maybe they figure out that they never really did love the other person, but the sex is good. Whereas some couples stop having sex for whatever reason, while remaining solidly together and very married.

So when is it that it ceases to be adulterous to have a sexual relationship with someone who has been in a relationship recently? And what about couples who only live together and never get married? Can they screw around all they want because they aren't legally married? It was a freaking ethical nightmare, one I couldn't get to fit into any of the mathematical or philosophical formulas I'd been given in my college classes.

Love was just too complicated. Maybe I had been better off as a sex-starved lesbian with a hot dream life. Dream sex was so much better because it wasn't complicated by all these relationship issues. Too bad my waking life had to have a head-on collision with my dream world.

Once I was back inside, I proceeded to lock the house up tight for the night. It was too weird to have a sheet of plywood for a window. I really liked that window. It helped to keep me from feeling claustrophobic in an otherwise relatively small house. Now I felt closed in, and I wasn't even closed in by myself. Maybe it would be better if Marie went back over to her house as soon as she felt ready to face it. Perhaps we could go over tomorrow after we made the phone calls we needed to make to get all the balls rolling.

Jolly was sleeping on the floor in the kitchen. I settled on the floor again next to her. "Hi, girl. It's been one helluva day, hasn't it?"

Her tail wagged a little bit.

"I'm glad it's nearly over, aren't you?"

More tail wagging.

From my position on the floor, I could see that there was glass in several places along the baseboards in the kitchen. I had only done a cursory sweeping of this room. I led Jolly over to the couch, which was relatively unharmed. There were black marks on one end of it, which I took to be tire marks. Now there was a story to tell when friends came over for a visit. Not that I had a lot of company. Tonight was probably the most people I'd had in my house at one time since I moved into the place three years ago. That was a sad state of affairs, I suppose. Except that I wasn't much of an entertainer, and I liked it that I had a few good friends.

Dave came over to watch sports sometimes because his wife absolutely hates them. He catches a lot of games at a sports bar near his house, but when the big events are going on, it's more fun for us to watch them together. Other than that, it was usually just Jolly and me hanging out, dancing to jazz, watching sports on television, reading, surfing the Internet. It was a quiet life, but a good one.

I got the vacuum cleaner out of the closet and plugged it in. Jolly jumped down from the sofa and went to hide in the spare bedroom. I pulled the dining room table out from the wall and vacuumed very carefully around the kitchen and dining area. I noticed a bunch of cobwebs on the wall that apparently managed to survive the crash scene just fine. I shook my head and started vacuuming the walls and corners.

When I got close to the refrigerator, I realized that there was glass on the top of it, neatly arranged in the dust that had gathered there since the last cleaning. It suddenly hit me again what it must have sounded like when that car came through the window. The sound of the window shattering must have been horrendous. It had certainly sent glass flying in every direction. There were even little pieces on the windowsill behind the blinds on the far wall of the kitchen. The physics of the whole thing was mind-boggling. My mind tried idly to construct a mathematical word problem from it. If a car traveling 30 mph passes through a plate glass window, how many years will it take to find every last piece of glass that went flying through the house.

When I was convinced that the kitchen was safe enough, I switched off the vacuum cleaner and called for Jolly to join me again. She came out rather tentatively. She really didn't care for the racket of the vacuum cleaner, but at least there was no glass on the floor any more. Or at least none that I could see at the moment. I decided to run a wet mop over it too to pick up any missed slivers. Jolly decided to watch my cleaning activities from the relative safety of the sofa. When I was finished mopping, I set the box fan up to blow on the floor, so it would dry faster. Otherwise I knew I'd end up with little doggy prints all over the kitchen. I set the fan on high about the time Marie emerged from my bedroom.

She looked at me as though I were a stranger. "What are you doing out here? It sounds like a demolition crew."

"God, I'm sorry. I didn't mean to disturb you. I noticed more glass on the floor in the kitchen and decided that I'd better be more thorough about cleaning that room. I didn't want Jolly to cut her paws on glass. I thought most of the glass would be contained in the living room so I didn't have the cleaners work in here. Apparently I was wrong. There was some glass on top of the refrigerator of all places."

Marie started crying again. "Oh Jill, I'm so sorry for all this mess. I should be helping you clean it up instead of lying in bed willing myself to disappear."

"What? No, I wouldn't let you help anyway. I'm not the one who just lost my husband. I can clean up the house just fine by myself. If I need more help, I'll call that cleaning crew back. You need to be doing whatever it is you need to do to take care of yourself."

"That's just it, Jillie. I don't know what that means any more. I don't know what I should be doing or feeling."

"I don't think there's any one way you're supposed to feel. You just feel whatever emotions are there as the shock falls away, and you're left with the reality of the situation."

Marie shook her head as though to clear it. "You make everything seem so logical. Aren't you ever at a loss?"

I walked over to her and wrapped my arms around her. "Yeah, I am. I'm at a loss right now because I don't have a clue what to do to help you survive this. Cleaning my house I can handle. It's practical and methodical, something my brain understands. My guess is that there's nothing I can say or do to make you feel better. But I'm here if you need to talk. I'm here if you need to sit and say nothing. I'm just here."

"Thank you. That means the world to me."

I kissed the top of her head and noticed that her brunette roots were starting to show. I hadn't realized until that moment that she colored her hair. I started to say something about the roots, but let it go, realizing that it was just small stuff that didn't matter.

Chapter 13
Making Arrangements

It was a really good thing that neither of us had to go to work the next morning, since I was pretty certain that neither of us got more than a couple hours of sleep. At some point in the night, Jolly got in between us on the bed and became a canine crossbar, so the three of us became a living letter H. I don't know whether she just needed to touch both of us at the same time to make sure everything was all right. I could imagine that she might be feeling a tad insecure after yesterday's cataclysmic events.

The first call I made in the morning was to Linda to see if she could help Marie figure out what she needed to do about tying up the loose ends of Enrico's life. Marie's first call was to Enrico's brother in New York. When Marie got off the phone, she started telling me about Enrico's background. I figured that it was good for her to talk about him, even if he had turned out to be a bit of a loose cannon that had exploded all over my house. The brothers hadn't been close in recent years, but Carlos was still pretty torn up about the sudden loss of his younger brother. Their parents had died long ago, and the two boys had been raised by the foster care system in New York. Carlos had made his home as an adult in New York, but Enrico had moved to California to find a better life for himself there. He'd gotten in a lot of legal trouble growing up, so when his girlfriend dumped him, he moved away to make a fresh start. That was when he met Marie.

Marie sat next to me on the couch. "Enrico stayed out of legal trouble after we met, but sometimes I felt as though trouble was still stalking him. When we'd go out, men who looked less than respectable would greet Enrico on the street. I never knew what to make of it. He claimed they were customers at the machine shop where he worked. I don't know if this was true or if he just said that to cover up how he knew them. It didn't feel like the truth to me. Sometimes he went out by himself and came back either drunk or stoned. He usually wanted to have sex after that, but he couldn't wait for me to get ready for it. He just plunged in and banged away at me. After a few times of that, I started using my fantasies to keep from getting so sore from not being open enough for him."

I cringed at this revelation, but Marie didn't notice my discomfort over her plight.

"I think he may have been dealing drugs because he always seemed to have enough money to buy things."

"What kind of things?"

"Like our stereo system and big screen television. Big, expensive stuff. I don't know. For all I know he was breaking into places and stealing this stuff. I really don't know how he got them. I don't think he made as much money at his job as he said, but he never let me see his paychecks. So I didn't know for sure. He kept a separate checking account for his money, and I kept an account for mine. We split all our bills, but he still ended up with a lot of cash on hand all the time.

"I hate to say this, Jillie, but part of me is relieved that he is gone now, out of my life totally. I never knew for sure when it was going to fall apart for him. I had this feeling that there was something wrong about the way he lived, but I didn't know what it was or what to do about it. If I tried to bring it up, he made some excuse about whatever specific thing I had mentioned. Then he'd tell me that he didn't need for me to worry about him. That he'd been taking care of himself for a long time, which was true. It was also true that he hadn't done a very good job of it."

Tears streamed down her face. I reached over and wiped them away with my thumbs and held her face in my hands for a moment. "I had no idea you were going through all this. You never let on that things were difficult at home."

"Oh, Jillie, I kept trying to pretend that everything was all right. I thought that if I pretended long enough, then maybe it would become true. The alternative was to leave him and face my mother's outrage and disappointment. I just wasn't up to it before."

I peered at her face. "Before? Does that mean that you're up to it now?"

"Now I don't give a damn what she thinks! Listening to her, being manipulated by her is how I ended up in this mess. I'm going to let her know it too. If she had just been more accepting of me as I really am, then I wouldn't have tried so hard to become someone I'm not!"

I sat quietly, letting her words settle into the woodwork.

"I know I could have defied her. I know I could have remained true to who I am, but I was hurting and instead of supporting me after Theresa broke my heart, she started harping at me about finding a man and settling down. I needed to stop flaunting this 'disgusting lifestyle' of mine in my father's face. She talked as though I was hurting my father by being lesbian. But I wasn't, and he told me as much before I married Enrico. He even tried to talk me out of marrying him, but I was resigned to my seeming fate at the time. I didn't have any fight left in me."

Just then the phone rang. It was Linda, wanting to talk to Marie. I handed the phone to her then went to the laundry room to start a load of clothes. When I returned, Marie was sitting on the couch with her hands in her lap. She looked like a scared little girl.

I sat down again next to her. "What did Linda want?"

"She was calling to tell me that she wanted to help me with all the arrangements for Enrico's funeral. But I'm not going to have a funeral for him. He wanted to be cremated anyway. I'll do that and ship his ashes to Carlos. I certainly don't want them. His brother can do whatever he wants to with them. But she's also going to help me with the paperwork to clear up any financial issues, getting me access to his bank accounts, etc. I don't even know how to begin to do any of that stuff. I'm sure glad Linda knows all about it. She's coming over here to take me to my house to look through his papers."

While she awaited Linda's arrival, I played with Jolly and tended the laundry. Marie called some places to see about cremation costs. When Linda arrived, I offered to go with the two of them to Marie's place. I figured I could start working on cleaning up Enrico's mess, while they worked on the paper end of things. When we got there, I was amazed at how similar her house looked to mine after the car incident. There was glass everywhere. The only difference was that there were no big pieces. Everything had been smashed to little bits. For the second time, I rolled up my sleeves and started sweeping and shoveling glass fragments into big trashcans lined with plastic bags.

Linda and Marie went to work uncovering Enrico's secrets. What they discovered was that there was probably somewhere in the neighborhood of $50,000 in his three bank accounts and a life insurance policy for $100,000, though it remained to be seen whether this would be worth anything given the questionable nature of his death. Marie was surprised to find out that the beneficiary on all of these accounts was Carlos even though they had been established after she and Enrico were married. While Marie was in a good financial state herself, she was taken aback that Enrico hadn't even planned to take care of her in the event of his death, even though she had named him beneficiary on everything of value that belonged to her.

Linda came out from the room where they'd been going through his papers. "I don't know what this man was up to, but he was definitely making money somewhere other than at his job. We found his pay stubs, and while he was making good money as a mechanist, it wasn't nearly enough to afford the lifestyle he had going for himself. I can't believe that he left all his money to his brother and left Marie with nothing except the house and his muscle car. Fat lot of good that will do her if she can't afford to make the mortgage payments. She says that she knew he must be doing something illegal on the side, but she couldn't figure out what it was."

I put down my broom and dustpan and sat on the edge of an armchair. I breathed out forcefully and shook my head. "I can't believe he'd do that to her. Better that he not have any money to leave than to have a wad in the bank that will go to his brother."

Marie came out from the room, apparently having heard me. "You know, I don't really care. He and his brother went through a lot together. It makes sense to me, knowing Enrico as well as I did, which I can see wasn't all that well. I'll let Carlos know that as soon as I give them all copies of Enrico's death certificate that three banks and an insurance company will be contacting him. It's okay, really. It's just one more confirmation that things weren't as they seemed with him."

I frowned at this thought. "Yeah, but you were legally married to the guy."

She shook her head. "It doesn't matter. I'll get his car and this house, and whatever money he had squirreled away here, which we've been discovering is quite a lot. I'll have to check the whole place over thoroughly to make sure he didn't have a stash in the basement or attic. Maybe I could pay Mack to go through the house with me. He's a detective. He'd know all kinds of places to look that I would never think of looking."

I shifted on my seat. "Hunh. Do you like his car?"

She frowned at me. "Of course not. It's a macho muscle car, but I can use it as a down payment for a new one for me since he destroyed mine. His car is actually worth quite a bit, I gathered from him. I may even be able to sell it out right and get enough money to buy a car outright with our discount at work. Then I could use my insurance money to pad my savings account while I try to figure out what I'm going to do with my life."

"Meaning?" I looked sideways at her.

"Well, I want to keep my job, and I make enough money barely to pay all the bills by myself, but that's about it. I would really need to sell this house and buy something a bit smaller with much smaller payments."

Linda nodded. "I know a good realtor if you need one."

I laughed. "Of course you do, Linda. You know everybody who is anybody in this part of the world."

She smiled at me. "I suppose I probably do. All those years of networking paid off." She winked in my direction.

We all looked at each other for a moment then went back to work. At one point, Marie emerged from the back room and handed me a bunch of papers.

"What's this?"

"Paperwork about the Mariners and somewhere in there are the passes. You can take it all home and sort through it. Recycle whatever you don't need. I really don't know what you would need anyway. But I do know that you'll find the passes in one of those packets or envelopes."

"Thanks, Marie. Maybe you'll feel like going to a game later on in the season. Just let me know."

"Not likely, but thanks." She rejoined Linda in her search through Enrico's papers.

When I'd finally finished sweeping up glass shards, I went looking for Marie's vacuum cleaner so I could finish the job of glass removal. I must've sucked up another couple thousand bits of glass and ceramics by the time I was through. I wound the cord on the machine and returned it to its hiding place in her hall closet. While I was in there, I got the bright idea to start checking Enrico's coat pockets. By the time I was finished, I'd come up with a couple joints, six assorted and unidentifiable pills, and just short of three thousand dollars in cash. I also discovered that the guy had a lot of coats and jackets. He must've had one for every nuance of Puget Sound weather, which is saying a lot.

When I'd finished my treasure hunt, I walked into the room where Linda and Marie were just wrapping things up and handed Marie the roll of hundreds I'd found in my foray into the hall closet. "I think these belong to you now." I put the roll in her hand.

Her eyes flew open wide. "Jesus, Joseph, and Mary! Where did you find these?"

"I have to confess that I've been being a bit of a snoop in the closet where you keep the vacuum cleaner. I found them squirreled away in all those jackets in there. Lots of pockets in them and nearly every one had one or two hundred-dollar bills. He had a couple of those hidden zippered pockets that held $500 each. God only knows where they came from, but I think that after we finish cleaning up around here, we should at least treat ourselves to a fine dining experience, compliments of Enrico."

Marie laughed and shook her head. "You remember when you were talking about my life being like a mystery novel of sorts with all this intrigue and drama?"

I nodded my head.

"It just got more so. There's so much about my husband that I just didn't know. I don't even think I want to know where this money came from. I hope it isn't counterfeit."

I took the roll back and held a couple of the bills up to the light. "Nope, these are not counterfeit. I can look at the rest of them if it will make you feel better. I don't know what slimy thing he might have been doing to earn all this, but at least it seems to be real money, and it may be the only positive thing you take away from this marriage."

Marie nodded solemnly. "You think it's okay to keep it?"

"What else are you going to do with it?"

Linda piped up. "Yes, I agree with Jill. I can't imagine that the police would be able to trace the money to illegal drug transactions anyway. If they could, what would they do with it, return it? If I were you, I'd just take the money and run, so to speak."

Marie shook her head in disbelief. "In that case, ladies, what are you in the mood to eat?"

Linda flashed a wicked smile. "Ever eaten at the Space Needle?"

Chapter 14
Up, Up, & Away

An hour and a half later we were seated at our table in the revolving restaurant overlooking Seattle. Some of the views were decidedly better than others as we went slowly round and round while we dined. We each ordered a glass of wine, some appetizers, and our entrees and sat for a couple hours until we were completely sated, and wondering what on earth we could do until one of us was below the state's alcohol level so we could drive home. At some point during the meal, Marie had ordered a bottle of wine because she and Linda had liked it so much. Since I'd had only one glass of wine, I was pretty sure that I'd be the one driving us back home again. We went back down to the gift shop to look around. We decided to buy the photograph they'd taken of us while we were eating. It had turned out pretty good, though I had to admit that Linda looked decidedly more inebriated than the rest of us.

We bought ourselves some useless souvenirs to commemorate the occasion of Enrico's passing and our discovery of a treasure trove in Marie's closet. Linda paused to phone Mack to see if he'd care to get paid to go treasure hunting at Marie's house. He agreed to it and told Linda to tell Marie to call him when she was ready. He warned her that he'd need to run a check on the serial numbers to make sure none of the money had been stolen from a bank. When Linda got off the phone, she relayed the messages to us. We all looked at each other guiltily.

I spoke up first. "So you mean we might be treating ourselves to a ladies day out with money taken in a bank heist? Oops."

Linda nodded solemnly then she suddenly keeled over laughing. She nearly knocked over the display she was leaning against.

I got a fit of the giggles just watching Linda totally lose it over this bit of information. She'd been so straight-laced all her life this scenario would have never occurred to her. Maybe it was because of the pills and joints I'd found in Enrico's jacket, but I was pretty certain that it was money made from selling drugs and not bank robberies. Not that it made it any better, just different. Nonetheless it was entertaining to see the effect it was having on my old friend who never did anything wrong in her life.

Marie looked from me to Linda and back again. She too burst into laughter. When I suspected that we were about to be expelled from the Space Needle gift shop, I grabbed the pair of giggling, tipsy women by the elbows and led them outside to get some fresh air.

It had been raining on and off while we were revolving our way around Seattle dozens of times, but the sun was out now and beckoning us to play. We looked like three crazy women who'd had too much to drink, jumping into the little puddles that dotted the area near the Space Needle. Marie suggested that we ride the Monorail, since she'd never done that before. So we did and discovered that there really wasn't all that much to it except a great view of Seattle, which we'd already gotten at the Space Needle. Then we walked to the nearest Starbucks and ordered lattés to help sober us up some more. Finally we decided that enough time had elapsed for us to drive home without fear of impairment. Or at least I decided that the little wine that I'd drunk had undoubtedly weakened sufficiently in my system. The other two were a different story. Since we'd taken Linda's car, I stuck my hand out towards her and said, "Keys, please, I'm the only one sober enough to drive home. I think you two are both way over the legal limit still."

Linda handed me the keys with a smirk. "Now what makes you think that you're more sober than I am?"

"Linda, you and Marie here drank three or four glasses of wine to the one glass I nursed through the entire meal."

"What? You mean we drank that whole bottle ourselves? That was a pretty big bottle." She looked at Marie as though trying to assess how high she was by looking in Marie's eyes.

Marie just nodded and started giggling again.

"Oh, god, come on, you two. Just trust me. You drank the whole bottle between you. I had just that first glass of wine we all ordered. You two ordered a bottle after you drank your glasses."

Linda put her hands on her hips and looked at me sternly. "I may have had quite a bit to drink, but I am certain that I didn't drink my glasses. They're right here in my purse." She pulled out her spectacles to prove her point.

I looked at her, then at Marie, and burst out laughing.

"Oh, brother, remind me never to let you drink again, Linda. You have no tolerance for it."

"I don't usually drink alcoholic beverages, but that wine was very tasty."

"Yes, I gathered that by the fact that you licked out the last glass," I said, trying to steer Linda back towards the Space Needle and our ride home. When we got back, I handed the keys to the valet who went to get the car. I pointed Marie in the direction of the pay booth for the parking fee.

She came back from paying and whispered in my ear, "How much should I tip the valet?"

I laughed. "You know, a couple bucks is fine, unless you really want to make his day, courtesy of Enrico's money."

She nodded and giggled again. She handed me a twenty and gestured for me to give it to the valet who was walking over with the keys. I took the keys and handed him the bill. "Have a nice day!"

We piled in the car, and I pulled away carefully. I didn't want anyone to think that I was drunk just because my companions were so obviously out of it. On the way home, Mount Rainier peaked through the clouds that had been enshrouding her. She looked almost as though she had thrown a white scarf around her base and gone for a ride in the sunshine.

When we finally arrived back at my place, Linda and Marie were starting to come down from their high a little bit. We sat on my sofa, lined up like ducks in a row. I no longer had a recliner, since it had been turned into a pile of matchsticks the day before. We had nowhere else to sit. Finally I got up and brought a kitchen chair into the living room. I didn't know how long anyone was going to stay, but it was looking as though the relaxing effect of the wine was kicking in, as the pair of them changed from giggly to morose. I was half afraid that Linda would need to spend the night here, but she suddenly sat up clear-eyed and said, "Well, I really should be off now. Goldfish and all."

She stood up, hugged Marie, and then told her to call her if she needed to talk over the weekend. Otherwise she'd be in touch Monday to help with getting the copies of the death certificates to everyone who would need one. Marie hugged her back very tightly. I smiled at them, decidedly happy that I'd introduced the two of them. Linda was providing the maternal support Marie was unlikely to get from her own mother, and which she so desperately needed at the moment.

I hugged Linda too and walked her out to her car, making sure that she really had sobered up. When I returned to my house, I knew before she said anything that Marie was going to go back to her house to stay. When I closed the door behind me, I looked at her and smiled. She started to speak, but I put a finger to my lips to stop her. "Let me guess. You're going to go back home now to sort out your life."

She nodded. "Things are a mess, Jillie, and I need to know what I'm going to do with myself now that I'm suddenly no longer married. I really care about you, but we sort of moved quickly in the heat of our passion and in our fear of Enrico. I'd like to have some time to myself before I decide whether we should start over and try to have a relationship at a normal pace."

"Mmm. I see. All right then. I'll help you get your clothes packed into Enrico's car unless you want to leave them here for now."

"Let's put them in now and I'll work on getting them out on the other end tomorrow. I'm too tired to unload tonight."

It took several trips with both of us carrying out suitcases, boxes and hangers full of clothes. When we were finally done, I hugged Marie to my chest then released her to the universe. It hurt to think that we'd done all that we'd done and gone through all that we had, just to let it slip through our fingers. But life was like that sometimes. Sometimes you wake up and find that the dream was just a dream that dissipated with the coming of dawn.

Chapter 15
All Decked Out

Saturday dawned bright and sunny as though the world was oblivious to the desolation in my heart. Part of me couldn't believe that Marie had just gone back home again, as though nothing had happened between us. I didn't even know if I should hope that Marie's time to herself would result in her coming back to me. All I knew was that she needed to be alone, and I needed to think about what had just happened. In the space of a week, my world had turned upside down, and I was still cleaning up the mess from the upheaval that had resulted.

I let Jolly outside for her morning run. I went out back to watch her run around like a crazy dog for a few minutes. I decided to sweep some of the winter debris off my really small back patio. While I lost myself in my gentle labors, I reached the conclusion that I should go ahead and build a huge deck back here. I had the coolest backyard in suburbia. With two huge maple trees perfectly spaced to provide maximum shade for the harshest of summer days, which were few and far between generally, I'd always thought that it would be cool to have a big deck that encircled each of the trees. After everything that had just happened, I really needed the mental distraction, so I started laying out a more complete design in my head.

By the time I'd finished my coffee, I'd decided to draw a diagram of what I wanted so I could head to Home Depot today to get the lumber. Since I was borrowing Dave's pickup anyway, I'd just go get the lumber at the same time. Maybe I could even get mister linebacker to help me build the thing in exchange for a Mariners game or two. I quickly sketched out a drawing of the proposed deck. I didn't want to cover all the grass, but I figured it would be better to landscape the backyard so it had less grass and more native shrubs to provide a natural setting. The less I had to mow, the better. My house was on a double corner lot so I had ample space to work with in creating my backyard paradise.

I drove my car over to Dave's house to get his truck. When I returned, I loaded the back of it with the bags and boxes of broken glass and the splintered recliner. My coffee table had managed to escape destruction by having been scooted by the recliner, out of the way of the flying car. While it had been scratched in the scuffle, it remained standing on all four legs several feet away from where it had been when I left for work that morning. I laughed at the thought of it trying to scurry away, like some sort of wooden crab, out of the path of the winged Honda.

After I'd dropped off the debris at the dumpster at work, I drove over to Home Depot to get the building materials I'd need for the deck. I ended up having to go back in twice before I felt confident that I'd remembered everything. I drove back home and unloaded the lumber and supplies then drove back to Dave's to get my car and ask him about helping me with the deck. When I told him about the Mariners tickets, he got very enthusiastic about the project for which I needed his help. When I told him they were box seats, I could all but see drool forming at the corners of his mouth. We decided to start today since the weather was nice and looked as though it might hold all day, so I went home to start laying things out and getting organized. Dave said he'd be over as soon as he mowed the yard and washed his wife's car.

Just for a moment, I wondered if I'd missed out on a good thing by being such a self-sufficient lesbian. It might be nice to have a guy around to mow my yard and wash my car for me. Then I thought about the three screaming kids he'd be leaving in her care while he helped me build a deck. I was certain I had gotten the better deal. I could handle kids as long as I could give them back to their parents before they got sick or grumpy. I was pretty sure that being with them all the time might just push me over the edge.

About the same time Dave pulled up, the phone rang. I waved him into the backyard, all the while gesturing that I needed to get the phone. I picked it up just before the answering machine would have gotten it. It was Mack, calling to see if I wanted to hang out and watch television or something. He had been planning to spend the day with Linda, helping her figure out how to stem the tide of goldfish deaths, but it seems she had awakened with a splitting headache. Something out of character for her.

I burst out laughing. When Mack asked me what was up, I told him that it would be easier to explain in person. Then I told him what Dave and I were planning to do, and I might as well have told him we were having a keg party because he was all up for coming over and helping us. So I invited him over to help with the same invitation of sharing the season passes so generously bequeathed to me by the dearly departed Enrico. I had to admit that he was rapidly making up for the pain and grief he'd caused me by running his car through my front window. I couldn't help but wonder if he weren't standing outside the pearly gates, dispatching angelic help my way to make up to me for the shitty things he'd done to me as a parting shot. Well, if that's what he was up to, then I hoped they'd give him a break and let the poor schmuck inside. If ever a soul needed a good dose of heavenly light, it was Senor Enrico Garcia. I wasn't about to hold a grudge against him anyway. That kind of stuff is hell on the karma.

I went out back and let Dave in on the good news that Mack was going to give us a hand today. I decided that I should run to the store and pick up a couple six packs of beer and some pizzas to cook later. Dave nodded in agreement and went back to aligning where the frame of the deck was going to be so we could get moving as soon as Mack arrived. Mack lived in Issaquah, so it took him a little while to get there, particularly since he'd stopped to pick up a case of beer on the way. I looked at the two burly men and decided that they'd probably be able to hold their beer a lot better than Marie and Linda had handled their wine the day before. I giggled just remembering it.

As we got going, I started telling the guys about the antics of the day before. Mack looked a little taken aback at Linda being drunk. Then he realized that was the reason for her headache today and decided that he would definitely have to give her some grief over that shenanigan. With the three of us working steadily, we managed to have the frame up and the decking about a quarter of the way finished by the time I stuck two pizzas in the oven to cook. I set the timer, raised the kitchen window so I could hear it go off, and went back to work for another twenty minutes.

We decided not to stop working to eat. I brought out the pizzas with some paper plates, napkins, and more beer. We ate a little then worked a little more. By the time it was getting too dark to see, we were nearly done with the basic structure. I went inside and turned on the backyard lights so we could see to finish it up. From the looks of it, all I'd have left to do was to build the benches around the two trees and put up the railings and benches along the sides.

I stuck a couple more pizzas in to bake and rejoined the guys who were laughing up a storm about something. I was afraid to ask, but I was hoping desperately that it didn't have to do with anything we might have done wrong on the deck. I had thought we were doing so well. I looked at them, hands on hips, and took the plunge. "Did we do something wrong?"

Mack shook his head. "No. Your friend Dave here was telling me about how hard it was for him to watch sports at his house. I let him know that my door is always open and all he has to do is bring the beer."

Dave gave me a big grin. I smiled, glad that these two guys were bonding so nicely over the building of my deck. If that would keep them working for a couple more hours, then I was all for it. I checked to see if anyone needed another beer. They both did. I went back to the fridge and discovered that we were down to the last six-pack of the case Mack brought. Thank goodness he'd brought it; otherwise we would have run out long ago. The timer went off for the new batch of pizzas about the time I'd gotten back inside from delivering the beers to the bears out back.

I brought out the next batch of food and plates. I looked at our handiwork and smiled. "Guys, you've both done an awesome job. I can't thank you enough. I can probably finish the rest of the stuff tomorrow by myself."

Mack grinned at me. "Ah, Jill, I'm game for another couple hours, even if this one needs to go home to his family. Just because it's dark doesn't mean it's late yet. Are you too tired to keep going?"

I smiled. "No, I'm good, if you're sure you don't mind."

Dave said, "Let me borrow your phone and I'll call my wife. I'm having lots more fun here. I'll tell her to order pizza to be delivered so she doesn't have to cook for the kids. She can have her sister stay for dinner so she won't be by herself. That way I can stay too to help get this finished."

"Okay, I'll go grab the phone. You eat and drink up and I'll be right back."

When I came back, the guys were laughing again. I was really glad they were getting along so well. I was hoping they would be able to get home okay. I was beginning to wonder if the alcohol was doing to them what so much less of it had done to Marie and Linda yesterday.

Three hours later, the deck was completed. There were cute little benches encircling the big maple trees and along portions of the outer railing. The steps were done and everything. It looked great, and the three of us had done it in one very long day of work. Okay, so they'd done most of it while I made sure that they were fed and watered. I'd done a lot of the decking work, but Dave was a master at woodworking, and amazingly enough, Mack had been able to follow his lead. I was so delighted that I went inside and got the season passes. I brought them out to the guys and gave them each one.

"Thanks, guys, you did a great job, and you deserve to have these. If ever one of you can't use a ticket, then let me know and I'll take your place, but you're really the ones who'll get the most enjoyment out of them. I'll probably take to sitting out on my deck every weekend now anyway."

They grinned at each other like two little boys with a secret. Then they each gave me a great big sweaty hug that I could have survived decades without experiencing. I told them to leave the mess to me, but to split up the beers and leftover pizza and take them home with them. Dave ended up going home with the pizza, while Mack went home with the beer. They both seemed happy and sober enough to drive. I figured they must've sweat out most of the alcohol during the afternoon. Dave didn't have far to drive anyway, and I was pretty sure that Mack wouldn't have driven if he'd been in bad shape. He seemed way too responsible for that.

As for me, I left the mess to clean up tomorrow. It wasn't as though the local raccoons were likely to take anything, since there wasn't any food involved. I got Jolly into the house and promptly took a shower to wash away the sawdust and sweat. When I came out, Jolly was already on the bed waiting for me. Apparently watching us work so hard must've worn her out. I petted her on the head and crawled into bed more tired than I'd felt in a long time.

Chapter 16
Nowhere to Go

Sunday morning arrived one slow drip at a time. "Darn. I'd hoped to get the deck stained today, but I guess that isn't going to happen now," I said to Jolly, while I looked out the window, coffee cup in hand. "Well, old girl, at least we got the thing built. How cool is that?" She wagged her tail a little bit. "Yeah, that's what I thought too. Very, very cool." I petted her head and opened the doggy door for her. Jolly exited without any excitement. I couldn't blame her really. I was awfully glad I didn't have to go stand in the rain to take a leak. I watched as she tentatively crossed the wet wood of the deck. Then I saw her stop and sniff the air around her. A moment later she was under the deck squatting. *Hmm. That seems to be a nice compromise for you.* At least it wasn't raining as much under the deck that was under the maple trees. Not that the maple trees had many leaves at the moment. Those would come later in the spring.

It never ceased to amaze me how huge the leaves were on these trees. Of course, they were called big leaf maples, but it seemed odd to me that a leaf could be a foot wide and a foot long. They should've named them "Big Foot Maples." *Sasquatch maples, that's what we should call them.* I snickered at my own silliness.

Jolly came back through the doggy door. "Hey, you. You're a little bit wet. Let me get a towel to dry you off."

Then, as though I'd just made her realize that she was indeed wet, she decided to shake, flinging a load of water droplets in every direction, including towards my face. "Thanks so much for that. You could have at least waited for your towel." I wiped my face on my shirtsleeve then reached into the laundry room and grabbed the doggy towel from the hook where I kept it for days such as these. I gave her a good rubdown then hung it back up to dry.

"So what do you think of the deck?"

She wagged her tail some more then walked over to her dish and looked up at me as if to say, "It's great. Now where's my breakfast?"

I got her some food then sat down at the kitchen table to ponder the blur on the windowpanes. It seemed oddly like a perfectly normal weekend for me, almost as though nothing whatsoever out of the ordinary had happened this week. Except, of course, that my recliner was missing, my front window was a sheet of plywood, and my couch was now sporting tire tracks. But every sign that Marie had been living here had been stripped from the place. Aside from the strange house anomalies, I could almost pretend that none of it had happened, and that I had not fallen in love with Marie. Except that now my heart was missing, and there were tire tracks left in its place from the speed at which Marie had driven back out of my life, spinning her wheels in her haste.

"I'd ask you, Jolly, what I did wrong, but I don't see how I possibly could've done anything wrong. I didn't have enough time and opportunity to screw up this relationship." Looking back over the week, I realized that we'd had sex for real only that one night when Marie had fled Enrico in fear for her life. Granted, we'd had a lot of sex that night, but it was still only the one evening. *Hmm. That doesn't bode well.* "Gosh, Jolly, I think I just had a one-night stand. How weird is that? I don't do one-night stands." She came over and plopped down at my feet. I was grateful that she wouldn't judge me for my lack of common sense. "Oh, I know, it was an incredibly stupid thing to do. She was married still, even if she wasn't particularly happy with him. Still, she was married. So, Jolly, forthwith I hereby decree, no more married women. I'm not allowed even to think about them in any sort of sexual context, and I am most especially forbidden to dream about them."

I wasn't quite sure how I was supposed to control the dream part, but I'd cross that bridge another day. Perhaps by stopping myself from thinking about a woman in the daytime would help me not to dream about her at night. At least it sounded good in theory.

"You know, Jolly, this would be a lot easier to do if I had someone. I'm mean, I'm just kind of a sitting duck here with no one to fill my thoughts by day or my dreams by night."

Just then the phone rang, so I wasn't able to explore these issues any further. I answered the phone, not daring to hope that it might be Marie. Good thing, because it wasn't. But it was Linda, so that was good.

"Jill, love, how are you this fine and dreary morning?"

I took a sip of my coffee before answering. "Okay, I think. I rather enjoy dreary mornings like these. And you?"

"I'm much better today. I can't say that I was feeling all that keen yesterday."

"So I heard."

"You heard what?"

"I heard from Mack about the splitting headache."

"Oh, dear. Why were you talking to Mack yesterday?"

"Actually, I spent the entire day with him. He and my buddy Dave came over and helped me to build my dream deck out back. I'd been thinking about doing it for a while, but never really got motivated to go out and just do it. For some reason I found the motivation when I was sipping my morning java on my back patio, basking in the sunshine that was so plentiful yesterday."

"Hmm. No playing footsies with Marie, having a leisurely morning of sex in the suburbs?"

"No, she left not too long after you did. Don't know if I'll hear from her again."

"Don't be silly, Jill, of course, you'll hear from her."

I took one last swallow of my coffee then rinsed the cup out and left it in the sink for later. I turned around and leaned against the sink while I continued talking to Linda. "I'm not being silly. She told me that she needed time to work through all her emotions and figure out if she wanted us to start over again and try to have a relationship at a normal pace. Something like that. So, no, I don't know if I'll hear from her again. Other than at work, I mean, and I don't know if she's going to take some time off to get her life straightened out. God knows we found enough money lying around her house yesterday to support her for a few months. Unless she has some secret heavy drug habit I don't know about."

"Don't be daft, love. Marie doesn't do drugs."

"How do you know that, Linda? Her husband was clearly into them. I found some pills and joints in his coat pockets too."

"What? You didn't tell us about those."

"No, I didn't. I shoved them in the pocket of my jeans while I was digging for more money. I forgot about them."

Linda tittered on the other end of the line. "Do you mean to tell me that you have pot in your house?"

I stopped and thought about that for a moment then laughed. "I guess I do at that. Would you like to come over and smoke a joint with me? I bet you've never done that."

"*Au contraire, mon chere.* I smoked pot a few times with my ex-husband."

"You're kidding me! You have always seemed so straight to me. All through college, you never even skipped a class to sleep late."

"I wasn't going to pay perfectly good money to go to college just so I could ditch my classes, and I didn't smoke pot again after I left my husband. I just figured that was one of the many ways that he'd been a bad influence on me. But you're not telling me that you're actually going to smoke that thing, are you?"

"I hadn't planned to smoke it. I hadn't planned to do anything with it. Still, it could be fun. I haven't gotten stoned since college."

"I didn't realize that you were into smoking pot in college. How did I miss that?"

"Mmm. That was after you had gone on to grad school. I sort of fell in with a bad lot for a little while. I came to my senses pretty fast and stopped hanging out with them before I ruined my brain and wasted my education."

Linda sniggered into the phone. "Hmm. You're getting to be quite a bad influence on me."

"Ha! I had nothing to do with your drinking binge the other day. You did that all by yourself without any encouragement from me."

"I wasn't talking about the drinking."

"What then?" I looked at Jolly on the floor and shrugged at her, not understanding what Linda was implying.

"You're the one who got me thinking about having sex with a woman."

"Oh, no. You can't tag me with that. You're the one who started thinking about women. Don't blame me for recruiting you. Besides, that would not be a bad thing. You've never actually slept with a woman, have you?"

"No, but it seems so sexy."

"Linda, all forms of sexuality are sexy. Being turned on by the thought of lesbian sex isn't necessarily an indicator that you're lesbian. It pretty much just indicates that you have a pulse. Do you feel attracted to any women in particular in your life? What about men?"

She cleared her throat and paused. "I guess I think about men most of the time, but I'd like to know what it's like to be with a woman."

"Okay, so you're bi-curious."

"I'm what?"

"Bi-curious. It just means what you just said. People put ads in the personals about being curious. That's usually a flag to me that a heterosexual woman wants to have a fling with a woman with no commitments. Then she gets to go back to having her regular relationships with men, thereby retaining her heterosexual privileges."

"That's rather harsh. Aren't people bisexual too?"

"Oh, yeah, totally. It's just that they end up in relationships sometimes with men and sometimes with women. That's different than looking for a fling with someone of the same sex. I mean, maybe those people are on the way to identifying as bisexual or lesbian, or maybe they're just interested in sex of another kind for a kick. I don't care what they're doing. I'm just not interested in being played. Hell, I think I just have been played, so maybe I'm feeling a little cynical at the moment."

"Jill, don't be so hard on Marie. She's really upset right now and probably a little scared."

"Why should she be scared now? Enrico is gone."

"It would be a little emotionally scary for anyone to go from building a life with someone to being alone that suddenly. She's feeling emotionally vulnerable, and I don't think she wants to recreate her last breakup. She married Enrico on the rebound from heartache. She told me yesterday that she didn't want to rebound to you without thinking. She wants to make conscious choices about anyone she gets involved with now. That's incredibly healthy of her."

I nodded. "You're right, but that still doesn't mean that we'll get back together."

"No, Jill, but it also doesn't mean that you won't. Give her the time she needs to figure things out. At least if she comes to you to start over, you'll know it's not a knee-jerk reaction to losing her husband."

I sat down at the kitchen table, resting my forehead on my placemat. I lifted my head again immediately and moved the placemat to find another piece of glass. "Shit!"

"What happened?"

"Nothing. I just found another piece of glass I missed. It was under my placement of all places. I guess I should clear the table and wipe it all down now. Sorry, I didn't mean to interrupt. You're right about Marie, and so far I'm doing really well. Yesterday I got up and decided to take charge of my life again. So the guys and I built a deck. It looks great. You should come down and see it."

"Can I wait until a sunny afternoon so we can have a barbecue or something fun? I can't stand the thought of driving all that way to sit and look out your window at the drizzle. I'm doing perfectly well here with my own view of grey skies and drippy weather."

"Yeah, rain check then."

"Now go flush that joint down the toilet before you get busted, and I have to bail you out of jail."

I laughed. "And who would bust me?"

"Mack for one. He is a former cop, you recall."

"Yeah, but I don't see him busting me for a couple joints. Geez, he and Dave drank at least eighteen cans of beer between the two of them yesterday. I would have been drunk and puking after that, but they didn't appear to have been affected in the least."

"Just because they weren't puking, Jill, doesn't mean they weren't drunk. I thought Mack was trying to cut back on his beer drinking."

"Maybe that is cutting down for him."

"Definitely not. He doesn't usually drink more than a six-pack on a day off."

"Still, even that seems like a lot. Is he an alcoholic?"

"I don't know. He really does drink only when he isn't working, but then he drinks a lot. Perhaps I should say something to him about it."

"Well, perhaps, but don't get me involved in it. I don't want him to get mad at me."

"Jill, love, he adores you. He told me as much. He thinks you're a lot of fun."

"Ah, so that's why he called yesterday to come hang out with me and watch sports on TV."

"Did he? I thought you were going to build a deck?"

"We did build a deck, but he got involved because he called me to see if I wanted to hang out with him. I think he was a little disappointed that you didn't want to spend the day with him."

"Did he say that?"

"He told me that you were supposed to be doing goldfish forensics together, but that you'd awakened with a terrible headache. So I let him know exactly why you had such a blinding headache."

"Oh, thanks, Jill. Now I'll never hear the end of that."

I snickered. "He indicated that might be so."

"Well, I suppose I should call him and make it up to him for standing him up for our goldfish date. I lost another pair, you know. I'm quite torn up about it."

"Yeah, sounds like it. Now go call Mack and start sleuthing to find out what's killing your fish."

"Okay, but only if you promise to flush those joints down the toilet. It's not worth endangering your brain just to try to forget about your heartbreak."

"I hear you. I'll flush it as soon as we get off the phone."

"I'll check back on that to make sure, you know."

I nodded into the phone. "Yes, I know, but this is why you and I can never be lovers. You have a tendency to act like an older sister to me."

"Oh, bother. Is that what ruined my chances with you?"

"That and the fact that I do think that you are truly heterosexual. And I think you and Mack belong together. Perhaps you just need to work on loosening up in bed."

"You really think so?"

"Yes, I do. You're heterosexual, Linda. Deal with it."

She laughed into the phone. "You're so charming, Jill."

"Go call Mack and invite him over for dinner. Then try fixing it in the nude, wearing only an apron. Welcome him at the door that way. Don't let him touch you while you're cooking. Then take your dinner to bed with you. Make him remove all his clothes. Then have dinner in bed without having sex until after the dishes are washed, with both of you still in the nude. See if that doesn't liven things up a bit."

"Oh, Jill, you are positively wicked. I love that idea. I'll let you know how it goes."

"Okay, you do that, only no details please. You're my older sister, remember?"

"Right. Bye then."

"Bye."

We hung up and I set the phone back onto the charger. "Now to wipe down the table, Jolly."

Jolly sat up, looked quizzically at me, and then yawned.

Chapter 17
Special Delivery

Monday morning rolled around, promising to be another dreary day. Donning my Gore-Tex jacket, I headed to work, armed with some phone numbers to call about getting my window and furniture replaced. Mr. Watanabe stopped by my desk to let me know that he was having some temps interviewed for Marie's position, since she'd called this morning to let him know that she'd be out all week and was considering taking a leave of absence for a month or more. I nodded, absorbing this secondhand information about Marie. It would have been nice if she had at least called and told me that herself. I didn't know if that was indicative of things to come or not, but I was determined not to dwell on it. I was going to make my phone calls at lunchtime and see about getting my house put back together. Then I was just going to move forward in my life.

I was definitely going to have to live by some new rules in my life. First and foremost was that I was going to start getting out more. Even if out meant only that I was going to take Jolly for more walks in the park. I could sure use the exercise, and I knew she got a kick out of being some place besides our backyard. Secondly I was not going to get involved with any more married women. Period.

That's as far as my list of new rules went. I never really cared for rules anyway, but I figured that having one or two guidelines for your life is a good thing. Too many rules might crowd out the fun in an effort to avoid any chance of experiencing pain. Having more fun in my life was worth risking a little pain, at least in theory.

The April days marched on in a relentless monotony of walks in the rain with Jolly. Every day we donned our rain gear and went for a walk in the park near my house. Okay, so maybe I was the only one donning the raingear. Jolly had only her fur to keep out the cold and damp days. After a week of this, I got my first ray of sunshine and a chance to sit on my deck under the maples. I moaned when the phone rang. Not wanting to disturb the solace of my coffee sipping and puppy dog petting, I picked up the cordless phone in the kitchen and returned to my deck seat on the bench under the maple trees. I was delighted to find that it was Linda and not a solicitor. Without perfunctory introductions, Linda launched into an account of her Friday afternoon adventures.

"Jill, love, I just have to tell you what a terrible, yet wonderful influence you are on me."

"Let me guess. You did the nude cooking thing with Mack, right?"

"Oh, yes, love, but that's not all. I decided to cook dinner for Mack last night, and since I didn't have a lot of pressing appointments, I left work early to give myself plenty of time to tidy up and prepare our meal. After I cleaned the house thoroughly, I stripped, showered, and put on nothing but my apron."

I tried hard not to picture this scene in my head, to no avail. I'd seen Linda naked before in college, so I had a pretty good idea of just how sexy she'd look in her apron, all soft and curvaceous, her creamy fair skin barely covered by the apron material. I cleared my throat noisily.

"What's that?"

"Nothing. Go on with your story."

"Mack was not due until six, so when the doorbell rang at four, I was a little surprised, but figured he'd just come over after he'd finished doing whatever it is he does when he's not working. I didn't even bother looking through the peephole, or I wouldn't have opened the door the way I did. Linda paused and started laughing. "Well, let me tell you, Miss Jill Michaels, am I ever glad I just swung the door open without a thought to my attire."

"Oh my gawd! Linda, you didn't. Who was it?"

She let out a squeal. "It was Christmas in April is what it was. It was the hunkiest delivery driver I've ever seen. His skin was exactly the color of milk chocolate. It was all smooth and creamy, and he reminded me of Denzel Washington, the way he was built."

"Oh my gawd!" I nearly dropped the phone in my vicarious embarrassment on behalf of Linda. "What did you do, you crazy woman?"

She let out another peal of laughter. "What did I do? I did what any healthy single heterosexual woman in need of a good lay did."

"You didn't!"

"I did!"

I shook my head in disbelief. "I so don't believe that my dearest friend and makeshift older sister had sex with a package delivery guy!"

"Well, you better start believing it, because I did, and it was the best sex I've ever had!"

"Oh my gawd!"

"You've said that several times now, Jill. You're going to have to come up with a better response than that."

"I'm almost afraid to ask how it all happened, but curiosity has got the best of me, Linda. What did you do with this guy and why was it the best sex you've ever had?"

Linda laughed naughtily. "How dear you are, Jill. It was the best sex I've ever had because it was completely anonymous. No strings. No expectations. No morning after. Just raw animal sex, pure and simple."

I shook my head again, trying to picture Linda being such a brazen hussy. "So what happened after you opened the door with your body bared to the world?"

"I'll have you know that my body wasn't bared to the world. It wasn't even bared to the delivery guy at first. You know what my apron looks like. It's got a bib in front."

"Yeah, and nothing in the rear!"

"I didn't have my rear to the door, you goon."

"All right, all right. Just tell me what happened. I can't believe you're telling me this." I got up and starting pacing around the maples in a bit of a figure eight to let off some of the sexual tension mounting in my body.

"After I got over the momentary shock that it wasn't Mack, and after I had the sudden realization that I was dressed as I was, something inside me switched to slut mode in a way that it hasn't since before I was married."

"Wait a minute! You were a slut before you got married? You never told me that."

"Not exactly, but I did have a few momentary slutty moments. But nothing quite like this—ever. I looked at the big box in his arms and said, 'Oh, that looks heavy. Would you mind bringing that inside and setting it down?'

"Then when he got inside, I shut the door and bolted it subtly. Before he could put the box down, I said, 'Wait! That should go upstairs. Would you mind bringing it up for me?'

"You didn't really say that, did you?"

"I did. I swear it, Jill. Then I ascended the stairs a couple steps in front of him, gliding sexily as best as one can on stairs. By the time we got to the top of the stairs, I could see with one quick glance at his pants that he had indeed enjoyed the view on the flight up.

I felt myself blushing.

"Are you red in the face yet, Jill?"

I laughed and felt my warm cheek. "I'd say I'm probably beet red by now."

"It just gets better."

I gulped, sat down, and patted Jolly's head a little too vigorously. She looked up at me in annoyance and went to run around the yard. "So go on before I burst with curiosity." I got up and started pacing again.

She laughed heartily. "Then I walked to the bedroom door and opened it. I went over to my bed and said, 'Here, let me just make room for you.' I went to the bed and leaned way over the end of the bed, spreading my legs as I did so. 'This should be a good place to start, don't you think?' Before I could say anything else, I heard the box hitting the floor, a zipper unzipping, and the rustle of clothing. Then I felt him. He leaned against me from behind and whispered in my ear. 'Get up on the bed on all fours, and let's see how that feels.'

"Then, Jill, love, he penetrated me smooth as silk. God, what a package he delivered. I must have been slicker than oil by that time and wide as the ocean. I think you might have been able to stick a telephone pole—"

"Stop, stop, stop, you're killing me! Don't say stuff like that. Just tell me what happened."

"You're so squeamish, Jill, dear."

"Squeamish? I don't think I'm being squeamish. I'm envisioning everything you're saying in my mind, and it's quite the picture. I just can't take the commentary about—never mind."

"You're turned on, Jill."

"Of course I'm turned on! It's you I'm picturing here. It's just a little hard, because I'm not used to thinking about you like this."

Linda laughed girlishly. "Oh, you are a dear, Jill, and here I thought you never thought of me like that."

I ran one hand through my hair, spiking it pretty good. "No, I had never thought about you in a sexual way before, but it isn't because it wouldn't have turned me on. It's just not a direction we ever headed in the past."

"And to think that I got you thinking about me that way right after I discovered how utterly heterosexual I really am. Though an exploration of a different kind might prove entertaining still."

"Stop it, Linda! You're making me nuts. Finish your story already."

"All right. So I crawled up onto the bed on all fours and we went at it like a couple of dogs on the street."

I let out a disgusted sound. "Oh now, that ruined it for me. How could you put it that way?"

"Well, that's what it was like. We were just a couple of animals having sex as though our lives and the human race depended on it. Then when it was over, he turned me over, kissed me with his big soft lips, and said, 'Why don't you order something else that needs a delivery some time?' I smiled and said, 'Yes, I just might have to do that.' Then he glanced at his watch and frowned. 'I've got to go, but I hope to see you again soon.' He kissed me on the nose, got up, pulled up his pants, and ran back downstairs. In a moment he was back for the signature he'd forgotten. I signed my name then collapsed in a heap of ecstasy."

"Oh my gawd." I ran my other hand through my spikes, making it even spikier if that were possible.

"Please, Jill, surely you can say more than that."

I shook my head. "No, probably not. I so cannot believe that you did that, and yet after your drunken binge at the

Space Needle, maybe I should believe that you are not the straight-laced woman I'd always thought you were."

"Does that mean we can have sex now?"

"No! Let me digest one thing at a time please. You can't tell me all this and then ask me to have sex with you."

"Why not?"

"Oh, well, how about let's start with unprotected sex. I'm guessing that neither of you happened to have a condom on you in that moment before he deep-sixed you."

"Six? Oh, Jill, love, he was more like a twelve."

"Linda! I'm serious. Did you think about getting pregnant or an STD?"

"No, Jill, for once in my life, I did not do the smart thing. I did the spontaneously sexy thing, and I'm not at all sorry about it. That was a once in a lifetime moment, and I'm glad I grabbed that bull by his horn and let him ride me for all he was worth."

"Oh, that's just great then. Hopefully there'll be no babies born from that spontaneously sexy moment and no painful, lifetime reminders either. But don't ask me to have sex with you after you just did that."

"I say, does that mean you'll consider it later?"

"Stop already. Just bask in the glory of your sluttiness for now and leave me out of this. I still can't believe you actually did that. You're not making this up, are you? You weren't taking a nap and dreaming it, were you? I've had some pretty wild sex in my dreams lately, so I'm willing to believe nearly anything can happen in our dreams."

"No, Jill, this really happened. Your dear friend Linda got laid and in a big way. A way that really opened her up. Mack and I ended up having sex that night too. Several times in fact. The delivery guy was just the beginning of a night of a new, sexier me."

"You had sex with Mack too last night? Wow! How can you do that?"

"What?"

"Have sex with two different men in one night?"

Linda snorted. "I really don't know. I just know that it felt good, and the delivery guy did me a world of good."

"Do you even know his name?"

"The delivery guy? No, of course I don't know his name. That would have made it not so anonymous. Though, he does know my name, since he delivered that box. We didn't really stop to chat before we had wild sex. You know, Jill, I've never actually had sex with a black man before."

"Well, congratulations, I guess. Was it that different?"

"Oh you know, it was very different, but I don't know if the difference was the moment or who he was. I think it was really about who I was in that moment, and I would've been just as totally a sex kitten if he'd been white or Asian or whatever."

"Sex kitten, huh?"

"Yes, a sex kitten. Of course, it didn't hurt that he reminded me of that hunky Denzel Washington. I'd have sex with him in the middle of a busy intersection if he wanted it."

"Stop it!"

"What?"

"You're making me crazy. I have such a bad case of cognitive dissonance. I can't stand it that my sweet, innocent big sisterly friend is behaving like a slut. I can't digest all this new information in one sitting."

Linda laughed. "I'm sorry."

"No, you're not, but apology accepted anyway. Just try to behave from now on."

"All right then, I'll try to behave, but I don't feel the slightest bit repentant."

"That's okay. Just don't say anything more. You've already told me enough for one Saturday." I sat down by the maples again. "By the way, it's a bright sunshiny day here.

Why don't you come over and have a cookout with me? You can bring your boyfriend, if you like."

"Delivery guy or Mack?"

"What are you talking about? If you don't know his name, how could he come with you?"

"Love, he came with me just fine yesterday."

"Linda!"

"Hmm. I'm still behaving rather badly, aren't I?"

"Yes, you are, and I don't think you're trying not to."

She sniffed into the phone. "All right, Jill, I'll check with Mack as soon as he awakens to see if he's up for a cookout with you. I can't imagine that he wouldn't be, since I don't think the Mariners are finished with Spring Training yet. You may be in luck."

"Wait a minute. You mean that Mack is at your condo sleeping? He spent the night?"

"Yes, why is that so startling?"

"Aren't you a little worried that he overheard you tell me that little story about your sexual escapades?"

"Of course not. I'm outside in my car talking to you on my cell phone."

"Oh, okay. That's good. So you two will come for a cookout today?"

"Yes, let's do it. Why don't we bring the steaks and you can provide the grill and the deck?"

"Sounds good, but shouldn't I get some beer for Mack?"

"No, absolutely not. He's in dire need of sobering up. I found out that he got pulled over that night after he left your house. It was a good thing it was a friend of his from the force, or he wouldn't have a license right now. His buddy made him get out of the car and ride home with him. Then he took him back in the morning to retrieve his vehicle."

"Oh no! He seemed so sober. Well, except for all the laughing he and Dave were doing. They did seem sometimes like a couple of schoolgirls giggling. I wouldn't have let him drive home if he had seemed impaired. I don't drink much, so I haven't a clue how many beers it takes to impair the functions of a big bear of a man like Mack."

"Less than nine, I suspect. Quite a few less than nine."

"I'm so sorry, Linda. I couldn't really tell any difference in him whatsoever. He seemed alert."

"Yes, he's good at hiding it, which makes him the worst kind of drunk. Anyway, his buddy made him promise to go to AA, so he started going this week. It's a bit of a touchy subject with him still, so please, please, don't say anything about last weekend."

"Okay, I promise. What should I get to drink then?"

"How about making some nice iced tea? Then we can pretend that it's summertime and we're all on holiday."

I nodded. "Iced tea then. I'll run to Freddie's and get some chips and dip and salad too. How does that sound?"

"Spot on, love. I'll ring off now and rouse Mack."

"Okay. It will be good to see you both. I've had a rather morose week. It will be nice to have company now that my house has been repaired. "

"It will be good to see you too, love. Ta ta!"

"Ta, er, um, bye."

I turned off the phone, danced a little jig of glee, and then went back inside to set the phone back on the charger. Jolly followed me inside and lay down on the floor by the table.

"Hey, you. Don't you want to go back outside? It's nice out there."

Jolly just sighed and closed her eyes. I figured that it must be time for her morning nap, so I left her to it and returned to the deck and my seat beneath the tree for a few more minutes before heading for the grocery store.

Chapter 18
Grilling and Chilling

The Saturday cookout with Linda and Mack was the one bright spot for the rest of the month. We sat out on the deck and grilled the steaks. I let Mack do the grilling, since he seemed to enjoy it so much. I made the iced tea and studiously avoided the subject of beer. While he cooked, I told Mack a few more times how much I appreciated the great job he and Dave did on the deck.

"It was fun, Jill. I had a really great day, hanging out with you and Dave. He's really handy with tools. I think he'll be a good sports chum too."

I nodded my head. "Yeah, he's a good guy, and he definitely needs some guy time every once in a while. I know he watches the kids a couple nights a week so his wife can get away. I can see how they'd both need that."

Mack sort of grunted in assent. "I've got a kid, y'know. He's grown now. His mother raised him. I wasn't such a hot father. Didn't turn out to be such a great husband either. I'm glad to know Dave has a better handle on it."

I nodded, digesting this information slowly. "Where does your son live?"

"San Diego, near his mom. His mother and I split up long ago, but I tried at least to contribute financially to his upbringing. I didn't do much else for him."

"Do you ever see him?"

"Oh, sure, every once in a while, I'll head down there for a visit, but I'm self-employed now, so it's not like I get paid vacation time."

I watched Mack as he turned the steaks over and listened to the sizzling sounds that came as a result of the juices dripping down onto the briquettes. The scent of the grilling meat must have reached Jolly's nose too. She suddenly trotted up and settled down beneath my feet.

As Mack maneuvered the beef on the grill, I noticed a slight tremor in his hands. I wondered if this was from the reduction in alcohol consumption. I also suddenly wondered how old he was. I had realized in the back of my brain that he must be a few years older than Linda, but I was beginning to think that he was quite a few years older. I tried to do the math with a grown kid, which led me to think that he might be ten or more years older than she. I glanced over at Linda, but she seemed to be engrossed in communing with nature, so I kept talking to Mack.

"So when did you leave the police force?"

"About three years ago. Had twenty years on the force. Loved the job. Hated all the paperwork that went with it. I have to do a lot less of that now. There's still some, but it's mainly taking my surveillance notes and turning them into a legible report to give to my clients."

Linda instantly interjected, "And I do that for him, which is why he is my hired guy when I need one. I do all his paperwork for free, and he does all my bodyguard jobs for my women for free. It's a lovely arrangement really."

Mack smiled, put an arm around her, and gave her a squeeze. "It's a great arrangement. I'm only too glad to do the bodyguard stuff her clients need, and she doesn't mind doing my paperwork. She's really fast with it too, so it doesn't take her long. I'm a hunt and peck typist, so you can imagine how long it would take me to type a few pages worth of handwritten notes. Plus the bodyguard work doesn't require any paperwork at all unless something actually happens. Like Marie's case. There was quite a bit to write up for that, in case it was needed later for insurance or legal purposes. That would've been a nightmare for me to do by myself, but I just told Linda what happened and she typed it as I talked. It was done in no time."

The steaks were starting to look like they were getting done, so I went inside and brought out plates, napkins, and eating utensils. I refilled everyone's iced tea and set up a folding table to hold the platter of steaks. I went back in and brought out a bowl full of leafy greens and some potato salad I'd gotten at the store. We were soon seated on the benches that wrapped around the maple trees, enjoying a hearty meal.

I behaved myself for as long as I could. When I couldn't take it any longer, I shot a glance at Linda, who was deeply immersed in the task of eating. "So, Linda, did that package you wanted get delivered?"

She coughed and nearly spit out the mouthful she'd just taken. Mack looked at her with concern. She looked at me with incredulity. I smiled and looked down at my plate innocently.

After she coughed a couple more times and took a swallow of tea, she finally responded. "Sorry. What was it you were saying, Jill?"

I shook my head. "Never mind. I got what I wanted."

When she shot an exasperated look, I merely smiled and barely restrained myself from bursting into laughter.

Mack was oblivious to our near hysterical undercurrent. Jolly padded up from the yard and settled at my feet, looking as though she thought that she needed to keep an eye on me and my antics. I patted her head and gave her a small bite of steak. She happily ate it and looked up at me with those puppy dog eyes that let me know that she would be happy to help me out if I had any problem eating any of that food up there on my plate. Having nearly finished it all, I slipped her the last bite of steak before taking my plate inside. I rinsed it off quickly and set it in the dishwasher for the dishwashing fairies to take care of after my guests were gone.

When I went back out, I found that Linda and Mack had both finished eating too, so I took their plates and silverware and got them ready for the dishwasher too. I started to go back out, but noticed through the window that they were sharing an intimate kiss. I smiled. I really liked these two as individuals. I'm glad they'd worked through their differences and had found a way to be a couple again.

Thinking about them made me think about Marie too. I wondered where she was on this fine and pleasant day. I wondered what she was doing and how she was dealing with everything that had happened. I missed Marie so much, and yet I also felt as though I barely knew her. As though sensing my distress, Jolly came into the house through the doggy door and jumped up on my leg to get my attention. I patted her head then leaned over and gave her a hug, as a tear rolled down my cheek.

Jolly licked my face, reminding me that she missed her too. Jolly doesn't have a lot of visitors, so having the attention of Marie, as well as me, had been good for her. I might not know Marie well, but my dog loved her too, and that said a lot to me. Animals are such good judges of character, and it was clear that Jolly trusted Marie. I got a doggie biscuit for Jolly and went back out to check on my friends.

Linda and Mack had started cleaning up the grill mess and putting stuff away. I think the kiss they'd shared between them earlier must have been a portent of things to come. They left soon after we had cleaned up, and I surmised that a little afternoon delight might be the dessert that was on their menu as the special of the day.

After they were gone, Jolly and I went back outside to sit on the deck. While I was out there, I realized that I would like to take a nap out here, so I got out my hammock and looped it on the hooks someone had embedded into the trees decades ago. The trees had responded by growing around the hooks, anchoring them even more deeply into the wood. I felt bad for the trees that someone had bored into them like that, but since they were there, I took advantage of them and sometimes slept out there beneath the two stalwart maples.

For some reason sleeping in a hammock that was connected only to these two trees created an intense feeling of being grounded and connected to nature. I had the best naps in this spot. I hadn't gotten my hammock out yet this year because of the weather, but I thought it might be worth it to drag it out today, even if the weather didn't hold very long. I could do with a nice outside siesta after all that eating. Once I was settled in my hammock, with Jolly beneath me, I fell into a most relaxed state of sleep that lasted a couple hours. When I awakened, it was starting to get cool quickly. Not being sure what was in the weather forecast, I went ahead and put the hammock back in the storage building to keep it out of inclement conditions.

Chapter 19
Park Place

As April drizzled the rest of the way into May, I wondered when we were going to come to the end of the rainy season. Finally another weekend dawned bright and beautiful again, and the deck dried enough for me to apply a coat of protective stain. I sat outside that night and watched the sun set over the houses in the neighborhood. I may not have much of a view from my backyard, but at least the backyard was looking better all the time. I'd planted a few more shrubs, since the plants didn't seem to mind me digging and planting in the drizzle.

Jolly got the hang of digging holes a little too well. She started digging them randomly in places around the yard. I filled the holes with more shrubs. When she finally stopped digging new holes, I discovered that she had designed a handy little obstacle course for her to run around on her morning jaunts. I had to wonder if she'd planned it that way, since she had stopped the digging again as abruptly as she had started it. I asked her about it later. She just looked at me, gave me a doggy grin, and wagged her tail a little bit. I took that as a yes. Then I wondered how on earth I was going to mow around this obstacle course.

By the time May came to an end, I'd pretty much given up on Marie. She still hadn't turned up at work and Mr. Watanabe hadn't heard from her either. I thought about calling her, but instead I drove by her house one Friday evening. There was a "For Sale" sign out front. It was listed with a realtor, so I jotted down the phone number to call later to see if they knew anything about the owner. I knew through Linda that Mack had never helped her search the house. I wondered if she'd found more money there on her own.

I'd also learned from Mack that Enrico was definitely involved in illegal activities. Mack had managed to sniff around his old place of employment enough to learn that not only was Enrico selling drugs for money, but he was also a male prostitute. He mostly did hand jobs and blow jobs for men, but he also had a few wealthy female clients that he'd been servicing. The guy had clearly been a sex addict, and it seemed that he'd turned his addiction into a lucrative sideline.

According to Mack's friends on the department, the police had been watching him for a while trying to amass enough evidence against him to put him away for a long time. I was a little shocked to find out that he had been so close to being arrested. It sounded as though Marie's intuition about him had been correct.

When I returned home, I got Jolly's leash so we could go for a walk to the park. It was still sunny out there, since the days were growing longer. The flowers and trees were really cranking up the amps on the beautiful displays they were flashing everywhere. When we got to the leash free area, I let Jolly go, knowing that she'd come back whenever she was ready to go home. I sat on a bench, closed my eyes, and breathed in the fresh air.

As my thoughts floated on the breeze, my brain drifted in and out of consciousness. I must have fallen asleep for a few minutes because my head was drooping down to my chest, until my ears picked up the distant sound of Jolly's ecstatically happy bark. My head snapped back up and my eyes tried to pinpoint her location from the sound of her barking. She seldom used that bark, so I had to wonder what was causing her so much excitement. In the distance, I could see her jumping up on a little girl. When I squinted my eyes to adjust for the distance, I realized that the little girl looked an awful lot like Marie, and they were now heading this way.

My heart did a double back flip and landed squirmily back into my chest. I sat up and leaned forward, trying to listen for something that would tell me what was going on. Finally I stood up and decided that if she were heading this way, the least I could do was meet her halfway. Just before we met, Jolly got distracted by a squirrel and ran off to chase it for a while.

Marie hugged me when we finally reached each other. "It's so good to see you, Jillie. I have so much to tell you. I've just come back from Yakima. I spent some time there with my family. I had it out with my mother. My father had to sit with us and act as referee, but it was good, very healing. We're starting over again, and this time she's going to have to accept me for who I am, and whoever I'm with. She agreed to that, amazingly enough."

"Wow! That's great, Marie."

She was nearly breathless from the walk and the excitement of her revelations. "Yes, and I'm selling my house. I want to get something much smaller. It doesn't make sense to have four bedrooms when it's just me. I don't know why Enrico wanted such a big house. Probably just because he could. I think he wanted to try to make up for how he grew up, which was basically without anything to call his own."

"I went by your house today and saw the sign out front."

"Oh, so they put it up already. That was fast. I just called them this morning about it. It was the name Linda had given me. I figured I'd have to get back into town and sign something before they put out any signs. Oh well, so that's starting."

"What about the money in the house?"

"I'm still going to have Mack help me search the house before I sell it. I found a bunch more before I went to Yakima. I've been living quite comfortably on it while I haven't been working, but I need to call Mr. Watanabe now that I know that I want to come back and live here and keep my job."

I tried not to look too hopeful. "So, you're coming back here to stay?"

She smiled at me. "Yes, Jillie, I'm coming back to stay. That's why I came here to find you."

"I don't understand."

"I went by your house to see you, but you weren't there, even though your car was in the driveway. I knew you couldn't have gone far. So I guessed that you might have taken Jolly to the park, since she was obviously not home either. The window and front yard look great by the way. You've been busy."

I nodded. "Therapy."

"Because of me?"

"Yes, because I missed you and didn't want to think about never seeing you again. I'm glad you're staying, even if you don't want to be with me."

"Ah, Jillie, that's what I'm trying to tell you. I'm coming back here because of you. I want to sell my house and get something smaller. Go back to work. See you in my off hours. We'll see where that takes us. But I want to try at least. I want to start over again at square one. I want to start having lunch dates with you again and flirting with you over deli sandwiches. I want to do that again, only this time without all my stupid complications."

"Wow! I don't know what to say."

"Well, I hope you'll say, 'I'd like that too, Marie.' I hope I haven't been gone so long that you gave up on me and found someone new."

I laughed. "No, I haven't found anyone new. I wasn't even looking."

She smiled slyly. "Actually I knew that. I've been in contact with Linda on occasion. I made her swear not to tell you, but also to call me immediately if you looked as though you were getting interested in anyone else."

I rocked back on my heels. "In your dreams!"

Marie reached out and placed one of her small hands on my arm. "No, not just in my dreams this time, Jillie. In my arms and in my heart. I want to be with you. I just needed to bury the past before I could even consider building a future. I hope you understand and can forgive me for disappearing from your life for a while."

I put my hands on her shoulders and rested my chin lightly on her head. "I understand and there's nothing to forgive. You did what you needed to do to take care of yourself. That's what I wanted you to do, even if it hurt in the interim. I'm glad you're back," I whispered into her hair.

Marie stepped back and pulled my face down to meet hers. Just as we kissed, Jolly came running over and leaped up at us as though she wanted in on the action too. We laughed and squatted down to do a group hug. Then we walked to my place to spend a little time talking together and catching up.

She loved the new living room furniture. I showed her my new deck and landscaped yard. "Wow, Jillie, that's some constructive therapy you've been doing. You've been making your world more beautiful."

We stood out back, arm in arm, admiring the lovely park-like setting. "I had to do what I could to make it more beautiful, since I no longer had you in it."

Marie looked up at me and smiled. "That's sweet, Jill, but I'm back now."

I leaned over and rested my cheek on the top of her head and sighed. "Thank you for coming back, Marie."

"Thank you for waiting for me to be ready to come back on my own terms."

We called Linda and Mack that night and made plans to get together the following weekend. Then I drove Marie back to the park where she'd left her car. She was driving a brand new blue Honda Accord coupe. We walked all around the car, looking at it. I laughed to see that she'd gotten her old license plates back from the wrecked vehicle.

"They actually let you have the plates off your old car? Usually the plates stay with the car, no matter who becomes the owner."

"They had to replace the one for the front because it was demolished. Mack helped me get the original specialty plates back to use on the new car. It was easier than I thought it would be. But now everything is back the way I like it with my car. I even have more features with this model."

I opened the car door for her. She turned and pulled me down towards her again. This time there was no dog to interrupt our passion. The embers that I'd thought perhaps had died out from a lack of oxygen suddenly burst into flames again. When we finally came up for air, Marie smiled warmly at me. "Call me."

I smiled back at her. "Should I wait until you get a chance to get home and settled?"

She shook her head. "Whenever you want." Then she laughed. "Maybe we can go to the Space Needle with Mack and Linda."

I just shook my head at her and grinned.

Then she turned her car around and headed for her house. I stood by my car for a minute. We were starting over, and I could hardly believe it. I looked up to the stars and breathed a prayer of thanks to the universe for helping Marie find her way, and particularly for helping her to find her way back to me.

I got back in my car and headed home to my dog, my warm bed, and a new future with Marie in it. I could hardly wait to go to sleep to see if she'd be there. In my dreams.

The End

Acknowledgments

I'd like to thank CreateSpace.com and Amazon.com for making their print on demand technology so accessible and user-friendly.

I'd like to thank my mother, once again, for her help in proofing and for being such a staunch supporter of all her children's and grandchildren's endeavors. You always gave us space and encouragement to follow our dreams. I think even you've been amazed at where those dreams have taken each of us.

Heartfelt thanks go to Belinda and Ginny for their early feedback and to Ginny, Belinda, Dr B, and Mom for proofing when I could no longer see the mistakes.

Thanks again to my dear friend Jan for being a friend I can depend on to make me laugh and to listen. But especially to make me laugh and laugh and laugh.

I have to thank my cats too—Dustin, Zuki, Bootsy, and Anjolie—for being the warm, loving beings you are. You keep me from getting too serious and from working too hard.

About the Author

Beth Mitchum has lived in the Seattle area since 1993. When she moved there, she finally was able to say, for the first time in her life, that she felt at home. Although she has lived in multiple places all around the Seattle area, her favorite nesting spot is on the Kitsap Peninsula, where she has been able to enjoy waterfront living and bald eagle watching for most of the time she's been there. Before moving to Seattle, she spent eight years in the Asheville, North Carolina area, a place of great beauty and folk art culture. The thing she misses most about living there is the great community of lesbians. You could walk into Malaprop's (a most excellent bookstore) in downtown Asheville and be guaranteed to run into several lesbians, many of whom she'd already know. Before moving to North Carolina in 1985, she lived in Lakeland, Florida, where she attended college, landed her first great job, and found the first of many really cool living spaces. Beth grew up in Winter Park, Florida, a uniquely European style city in the heart of Central Florida.

Follow Beth's work at UltraVioletLove.com and BethMitchum.com. You can write to her at beth@bethmitchum.com. Her other books are easily attainable at Amazon.com, where you can order autographed and personalized copies through bookshopwithoutborders@gmail.com You can also order directly from the author at the same email address. For a totally different take on her writing, you can read her blogs in the Amazon.com author profile section or at bethmitchum.com.

Titles by Beth Mitchum

bethwor(l)ds: 20 years of poetry

Driftwood
Driftwood: The Music (companion music CD for the novel, Driftwood)

Higher Love
In My Dreams
Naked on the Beach (forthcoming)
If Wishes were Horses (forthcoming, working title)

The Goddess Series:

Artemisian Artist
Gaia's Guardian
Demeter's Daughter (forthcoming)
Hestia's Healer (forthcoming)

Also look for the forthcoming poetry series UltraVioletLove Presents:

Sappho's Corner, Volume 1
The Poetry of Jae Dee (working title)

2149992